Finding Forever

FINDING FOREVER

PREVIEW ACCIDENTALLY FOREVER

Copyright © 2024 by Kathryn Kaleigh

All rights reserved.

Written by Kathryn Kaleigh.

Published by KST Publishing, Inc., 2024

Cover by Skyhouse24Media

www.kathrynkaleigh.com

No part of this book may be reproduced in any form or by any electronic or mechanical means, including information storage and retrieval systems, without written permission from the author, except for the use of brief quotations in a book review.

This is a work of fiction. Any names, characters, places, or incidents are products of the author's imagination and used in a fictitious manner. Any resemblance to actual people, places, of events is purely coincidental or fictionalized.

ALSO BY KATHRYN KALEIGH

Contemporary Romance

The Worthington Family

The Princess and the Playboy

Accidentally Forever

Finding Forever

Forever Vows

Our Forever Love

My Forever Guy

Out of the Blue

Kissing for Keeps

All Our Tomorrows

Pretend Boyfriend

The Forever Equation

A Chance Encounter

Chasing Fireflies

When Cupid's Arrow Strikes

It was Always You

On the Way Home to Christmas

A Merry Little Christmas

On the Way to Forever

Perfectly Mismatched

The Moon and the Stars at Christmas

Still Mine

Borrowed Until Monday

The Lady in the Red Dress

On the Edge of Chance

Sealed with a Kiss

Kiss me at Midnight

The Heart Knows

Billionaire's Unexpected Landing

Billionaire's Accidental Girlfriend

Billionaire Fallen Angel

Billionaire's Secret Crush

Billionaire's Barefoot Bride

The Heart of Christmas

The Magic of Christmas

In a One Horse Open Sleigh

A Secret Royal Christmas

An Old-Fashioned Christmas

Second Chance Kisses

Second Chance Secrets

First Time Charm

Three Broken Rules

Second Chance Destiny

Unexpected Vows

Begin Again

Love Again

Falling Again

Just Stay

Just Chance

Just Believe

Just Us

Just Once

Just Happened

Just Maybe

Just Pretend

Just Because

Finding Forever

THE ASHTONS

FOREVER AND EVER

KATHRYN KALEIGH

Chapter One

Charlotte Ashton

After parking in the lot two blocks from the downtown university offices, I stopped by the coffee shop and ordered two lattes. One for me and one for my best friend Zoe.

While I waited, I stood at the window and watched the midmorning traffic. Mostly foot traffic. Some cars stopped at the traffic light. People waiting at the bus stop.

A food truck parked across the street at the corner had a line six deep. Their breakfast burritos were well worth the wait. Zoe and I ate there at least once a week. Sometimes two. Sometimes for breakfast, but usually for lunch.

The end of August, the beginning of the school year, was my favorite time of year.

Anything was possible.

I had one class this term, an art lab really. So far six students had signed up. Advanced students who didn't need much more than some guidance and inspiration. I would take them down to the point before it got too cold. Let then spend some time capturing the rivers and the hills. Some would add people to their paintings. Some would not.

Even though I only taught one class a semester now, my love of the beginning of the Fall semester hadn't faded.

New year. New school clothes. New school supplies.

Maybe not the school clothes and school supplies so much anymore, but it was still a brand new year. Anything was possible.

Even though I worked all year round now, I still got that feeling of excited anticipation this time of year.

Maybe I'd stop by one of the shops after work. See about getting a new outfit. Maybe a new jacket.

We still had a week before classes actually started. This week was for meetings. For getting everything set up and ready.

"Char." I'd gone to school with Bradley. He owned the coffee shop now, but you wouldn't know it. He looked like just another barista and worked harder than any of his employees.

"Thanks, Brad." I took the coffee he'd packed up in a little cardboard carrier.

"I threw in a couple of muffins for you," he said with a little wink.

"Aw. Thanks Brad." I'd add a tip to his virtual tip jar when I got to the office.

"See you tomorrow?" he asked.

"Yet bet."

I stepped outside into the warm sunlight. In typical Pittsburgh fashion, the sun was warm and the breeze was cool. The skies were blue with just a few white wispy clouds.

Perfect weather.

Going up the three brick steps, I opened the heavy wooden door to the university's downtown office—an old sturdy brick building. One of those big four story historical buildings that had been here for centuries. The kind of building that had been built to last.

Even though it had been purchased by and repurposed for the university, it remained protected by the historical society. As such, it had no elevator. I walked up the eight flights of stairs. I went up and down several times a day and deemed it my exercise.

Zoe wasn't in yet, so I left her coffee and muffin on her desk. Before I sat down at my own desk, Dr. Reginald Jones stepped out of his office. He was a lean man, in his fifties, always clean shaven. Always wore a gray suit and tie that matched the streaks in his hair that some men had to pay good money for. He was a single man and we had never known him to date anyone. He was the most private person I knew and yet faculty and students liked him. It was doubtless due to his accommodating nature. If he could make something right for someone, he would do it.

"Good morning, Charlotte," he said, removing his glasses to look at me.

"Good morning," I said as I set my coffee and muffin on my desk.

Dr. Jones, Dean of the college of Arts and Sciences, was not known for his overt friendliness. In fact, most days, I didn't even see him other than in passing.

Something was different today.

"Everything okay?" I asked.

"I need to talk to you about something," he said. "You got a minute?"

"Of course."

I unwrapped my leather book bag off my shoulders and set it on my desk. Then, grabbing up my coffee cup, I took it with me as I followed Dr. Jones into his office.

My stomach felt tight even though I couldn't think of anything I had done that might get me in trouble. It had been a quiet summer.

Maybe he wanted to change my teaching schedule. If someone quit at the last minute, he'd need someone to cover their classes. That had happened before and we all pulled together.

If someone had quit, I hadn't heard about it yet.

Still trying to sort through what might have happened, I sat down across from him.

Dr. Jones' desk never had anything on it other than what he needed at any particular moment. He even kept his computer on the console behind him when he wasn't using it.

Right now all he had was his cell phone sitting on its charger on his desk.

As he checked something on his phone, I took the first sip of my coffee.

If someone had quit, Dr. Jones would have met with all of us at once. Or, even more likely, he would have sent an email. This had to be something more personal.

Just an assignment. It was just something he needed me to do.

I had no reason to be nervous.

It was just Dr. Jones usually sent his assignments via email and he wasn't a fan of meetings. Another reason why the faculty and staff liked him.

He steepled his fingers together and looked at me.

"Do you remember reading about the university adding on some satellite campuses?"

"Yes. Of course." An assignment. "I didn't think that had gone anywhere."

"They're still working on it. But in the meantime, they have decided to do a pilot study as such."

"A pilot study."

"Most of the details are worked out and they have a dozen students signed up to participate. To take classes."

Why did I not know about this?

As the assistant director of the college of arts and sciences, I should know these things.

I lifted my chin a notch. He was telling me now.

"What can I do?" I asked with more than a little relief. I could handle assignments. I was good at assignments.

And I had a new graduate student named William starting tomorrow. I knew William. He was a motivated and dependable student. Whatever it was, we could get it done.

"The pilot study is in Whiskey Springs, Colorado."

"Oh." I sat back. "Why?"

Colorado was a long way from Pittsburgh. A very long way.

"We had an unexpected benefactor throw some money at the program. Enough money to make things happen. He specifically requested Whiskey Springs."

"Why?"

Dr. Jones waved a hand in no particular direction and sat back in his own chair, lacing his hands behind his back.

"So what do we need to do?" I asked, straightening in my chair. "Secure a location? Scheduling?" These were all things I excelled at. My scheduling skills had gotten me promoted from associate professor to the youngest assistant director of the college of arts of sciences.

Shaking his head, Dr. Jones braced his hands on his clutter free desk.

"I need you to go. You've been chosen to run the program."

"Me? Why?"

"The benefactor specifically requested you."

"I don't understand." I pressed a hand against my brow.

"Before you ask," he asked. "The benefactor asked to remain anonymous."

"Why?" I asked, beginning to sound like a broken record.

I held up a hand. "I know. You can't answer that."

"Wish I could."

"So it's settled?"

"Yes."

"When do I leave?"

"In two days."

"Is this up for discussion?" I shook my head as I asked. I already knew the answer.

We wouldn't be sitting here having this discussion if it was.

Chapter Two

BRADFORD TORRES

After doing an external check of the Phenom, I boarded the private jet and sat down in the pilot's seat to start the preflight checklist.

The scent of jet fuel blended with the scent of new leather. The Phenom was new with just a few miles on it. I was about to add a few more.

I was early.

It was that perfect time of day when the sky lightened before the sun came over the horizon.

The sky was clear with just a few wispy clouds scattered here and there.

I opened up my iPad and checked the radar. Smooth sailing from here to Whiskey Springs.

This was a quick turnaround from my flight in from Houston

last night. Fairly last minute, but I was used to that. Last minute was my way of life.

But like most pilots, I rarely turned down a flight.

The saying I'd heard around the Skye Travels office was that flights were like catnip for pilots. Just dangle a flight in front of us and we'd follow you anywhere.

It wasn't all that far from the truth.

This particular flight was different though.

Noah was housing me in Whiskey Springs until further notice.

Further notice usually meant until someone needed a flight out.

At any rate, I'd brought my suitcase packed with enough clothes to last me a couple of weeks.

I liked to be prepared.

I checked the manifest.

Two souls listed in addition to mine.

Dr. Charlotte Ashton and William Barnes.

With everything done, I was ready to go. I sent my parents a text telling them where I would be. It was mostly just a habit. It wasn't that they were concerned about my whereabouts.

My mother, a writer, had hit the literary jackpot with her cozy mystery series. She and my dad had taken advantage of the situation as most people would, but not like most people, who could suddenly work from anywhere.

They had packed up and moved to Australia, leaving me and my sister here in the states. I halfway—maybe more than halfway—expected my sister to follow them, but she hadn't yet.

Me? No way. I was an American boy through and through.

Besides, I had the best job I could imagine flying for Skye Travels. It was hard to get on with Noah Worthington and I wasn't about to give that up just because my parents were having some kind of midlife crisis.

Still. They were my parents and I liked to keep them informed of my whereabouts.

I checked the time. My passengers would be arriving at any time.

I went to the door of the cabin and looked out. The sun was warm and the breeze was cool. That was one of my favorite things about northern climates.

Born and bred in Houston, I was accustomed to the heat. Didn't mean I liked it.

It was hot from March until October. Sometimes longer.

Anytime I could get away from that heat, I considered myself fortunate.

A taxi drove out on the tarmac toward the airplane.

I didn't see that very often. Typically my passengers arrived in limos. A person who could afford to fly private could afford a limo driver.

The taxi stopped next to the plane and three doors opened. The driver and the two back doors.

One had to be the young man, William. The woman who got out on the other side had to Dr. Ashton.

Not at all what I was expecting. When I'd been told they were affiliated with a university, I'd pictured someone much different.

I expected a couple of middle-aged people.

I had not expected one of my passengers to look like a fairy princess.

Not that she was dressed like a princess. She was wearing a pencil skirt with a matching blazer. Very professional.

But it was her slim figure and her hair that gave her away.

She was no ordinary university administrator or faculty. Not an ordinary person, in fact.

She had barely stepped out of the taxi when it hit me like a ton of bricks.

I wanted to date her.

The taxi driver pulled three suitcases out of the trunk.

The young lady, Dr. Charlotte Ashton, already had a leather book bag over her shoulders. Now she was rolling two suitcases toward the plane.

This would not do.

I bounded down the stairs and headed straight for her.

"Let me help you with these," I said, taking her two suitcases from her.

"Thank you," she said with obvious relief.

"I can take your bag, too," I said, holding out a hand.

"It's okay…" But she pulled it off her shoulders and handed it to me.

The taxi driver got back inside his car and took off. Just one of many reasons why my passengers hired drivers. A good driver always made sure their passenger not only made it to the airplane, but that all their luggage got loaded up properly.

Securing her bag over my own shoulders, I rolled her luggage to the plane and, while she watched, I slid it into holding.

Turning around, thinking to introduce myself, I found Charlotte with her back to me, talking quietly with William.

William was younger and had the lean look of a student. Carrying a backpack, he wore blue jeans and a lightweight jacket that looked at least one size too big for him. Taller than Charlotte, he bent his head close as they spoke.

"Ready to come aboard?" I asked, as I neared them.

"Yes. Thank you." Charlotte smiled. The smile lit up her whole face. My gaze was drawn first to her bow shaped lips and perfect white teeth.

Her green eyes, reminding me of a verdant forest at night with moonlight glowing through the leaves, were framed with dark, thick lashes.

With high cheekbones, her features were delicate, like the fairy princess that had been my first impression.

Although she wore heels, she was a full head shorter than me.

A gust of wind caught a strand of hair and tossed it across her face.

Tucking it back, she licked her lips.

"We're ready," she said.

Reaching the steps leading up into the airplane, I held out a hand to assist her up. I'd done it a thousand times for a thousand different ladies.

She put her delicate hand in mine and I knew this time was different.

Chapter Three

CHARLOTTE

Some might think it odd that since I had two brothers and one brother-in-law who were private pilots for Skye Travels that I would have had the opportunity to fly on private jets.

Such an assumption, though, would be erroneous. I had never had the occasion to fly on an airplane, private or commercial.

I was the quiet one of the family. I had one younger sister and three older brothers. All of them extraverted with strong personalities.

Since I preferred to stay to myself, spending my days drawing and painting mostly, when I wasn't at work, I tended to recede into the background.

I didn't mind. But here I was, a twenty-eight-year-old who had never flown in a private airplane. The worst part? Everyone assumed that I had.

I could have if I had pushed it even a little. But my family didn't push me. They left me to my own devices. So I had gotten my Ph.D. and now I helped others achieve their dream of painting and drawing.

Art was my life.

At the moment, however, I found myself in a rather odd place. I knew all about flying. I listened at the dinner table when my brothers talked about what they did.

Standing here beside the airplane, even William, my newly assigned graduate assistant and former student, assumed that I had experience in flying.

Why wouldn't I? Why wouldn't a twenty-eight-year-old Ph.D., assistant director of the college of arts and sciences have experience flying on an airplane?

I decided in one of those split-second moments when such things had to be decided that I wouldn't reveal my inexperience with flying. With what I knew about flying, it would be easy enough to pull off.

Should be.

Looking up toward the airplane door, though, I experienced a wave of anxiety. The steps were not what I had expected. They were narrow and they did not look nearly sturdy enough. Besides that, I was wearing heels.

Why hadn't I known not to wear heels?

Perhaps I should have consulted with my sister who was married to a pilot or even one of my two sisters-in-law married to pilots. They would have been happy to share their knowledge with me.

It was simply my lack of experience with flying. I was like the person who knew all about art. Had even seen photographs of great pieces of art. But had never seen one of those paintings in person. Never saw the texture or the layers on great paintings. And certainly had never picked up a paint brush.

The pilot came to my rescue. Yet again.

He had taken my luggage and stashed it in the plane's holding area. He had also taken my leather book bag. Under normal circumstances, my book bag wasn't a problem. But today I had an iPad, a notebook computer, and a ton of art supplies—in addition to the ones in my luggage, and a couple of books.

To say the least, it was heavy. It was with utmost relief that I handed it over to him.

And now, looking up the narrow steps to the door of the airplane, the pilot came to my rescue a second time.

Deep in my own thoughts, as I typically was, I had barely noticed him.

But when I put my hand in his, I looked at him. I *really* looked at him.

He was dressed in a black pilot's uniform—slacks and a blazer—and a cap.

He was a head taller than me and he was handsome in a city boy way with a touch of ruggedness. High cheekbones. Lips curved with amusement. But no one would ever accuse him of being a metro male. He didn't look like he had shaved this morning. He wore that slightly rugged five o'clock shadow and he wore it with style.

But his eyes stopped me in my tracks. His blue eyes grabbed hold of me and pulled me right in. They sparkled like a clear blue sky after a rain.

His hand was strong and any doubts I had about my ability to navigate the stairs in my heels vanished.

"Whoever designed these stairs didn't think about heels," he said.

"No," I said, smiling back. "They didn't, did they?"

"You go ahead. I'll be right behind you."

With one hand in his, the other on the steel railing, I stepped onto the first step. As I stepped to the second, true to his word, he was right behind me.

I reached the top of the stairs and stepped inside the airplane cabin.

It smelled new. Like a new car.

"You can sit anywhere you like," he said.

"Okay."

William followed, taking the first seat he came to and immediately turned his attention to his phone.

Was I the only one slightly intimidated by this experience?

I sat down across the aisle from William and watched the pilot press a button to bring up the stairs, then secure the door.

He turned around, glanced at William, then smiled at me.

"Come with me," he said, holding out a hand again.

"Why?"

"I have a much better seat for you than this."

I stood up and put my hand in his.

This was becoming a habit.

And I didn't even know his name.

Chapter Four

BRADFORD

This day was going a whole differently than I had expected.

When I'd gotten up this morning, I'd thought I was going to be flying a couple of academics out to Colorado. Routine flight.

I was only half right. Not even half. I was flying academics out to Colorado, but this was not routine.

My passenger, Charlotte, was the most beautiful woman I had ever seen.

Dark hair. Smooth pale skin.

I maintained my impression that she looked like a fairy princess.

One of the things I loved about flying was the time I got to spend with my own thoughts. As such, I rarely invited passengers to sit up front with me. I would let them if they wanted to, but I rarely invited them.

Charlotte was the exception.

I got her settled into the copilot's seat then sat down next to her.

She watched everything I did.

After I buckled myself in, she toyed with her own four-point harness.

"Need some help?" I asked.

"So it seems," she said, frowning at the belts.

I laughed.

"It can be quite complicated. Here let me help you."

Leaning close to her, I took my time with her harness.

She smelled like jasmine. A delicate scent that fit her delicate appearance.

"All set," I said when I had her safely harnessed in.

"Thank you." She looked over at me. "I'm Charlotte."

"And I have terrible manners. I'm Bradford Torres and I'll be your pilot today."

That brought a smile to her lips.

I loved her smile. I could already see that I would be doing anything I could to keep her smiling.

I put on my headset and spoke to the control tower.

"Cleared to taxi." The voice came through loud and clear.

"Ready?" I asked Charlotte.

"I think so," she said, giving her seat belt a little tug.

I handed her the extra set of headphones.

"You can wear these," I said.

A lot of girls wouldn't wear the headphones. They didn't like messing up their hair.

But Charlotte, looking charmingly delighted, didn't hesitate to put them on.

"Do you fly a lot?" I asked her as I taxied out to the runway.

"No," she said, looking away.

If she was going to say anything else, I missed it. The control tower came through giving us an all clear for takeoff.

After lining up on the runway, I gave the windsocks a final check, then took off.

As we achieved ground effect, I glanced over at Charlotte.

She was looking straight ahead, but she was gripping the seat with both hands.

Either she was a nervous flyer or she had never flown in a private plane before.

From the way she watched everything I did, I was inclined to go with the second option.

But could be both.

Either way, I sought to distract her.

"Your first time to Whiskey Springs?"

"Yes," she said, keeping her eyes straight ahead.

Since she obviously was not inclined to talk at the moment, I let her be.

We had plenty of time for conversation ahead of us.

Chapter Five

Charlotte

Our pilot, Bradford, handled the airplane with obvious experience.

I had not expected him to invite me to sit up front in the cockpit with him.

But I was quite happy about it. I knew enough to have a general idea of what he was doing, but I certainly couldn't have done it myself.

I knew the moment the airplane left the ground. There was that moment of sheer weightlessness.

I'd never felt anything like it.

I gripped the seat with both hands.

Bradford asked me if I'd flown a lot.

The answer, of course, was a definitive no, but I wasn't ready to tell him that yet.

I would tell him. Just not yet.

I didn't want him sending me back to the cabin.

We flew through a bank of wispy white clouds and I almost forgot to breath.

I knew there was radar to tell us if another airplane was nearby, but flying blind in the clouds made me want to close my eyes and hope we didn't fly into another airplane.

I didn't want to be a nervous flyer. In fact, I refused to be a nervous flyer.

I came from a family of pilots.

My Uncle Noah, in fact, owned this airplane and the airline it was part of.

He had started Skye Travels with just one airplane, then he had grown it into the most successful private airline company in the country.

I had met Uncle Noah, but he had come into our lives only a few years ago.

Most people would think it odd that I had never flown when my uncle owned airplanes—lots of airplanes. A whole fleet of airplanes all around the country.

Airplanes that two of my brothers, in fact, flew on a regular basis.

So, for the moment, at least, I kept all that information to myself.

We reached altitude and the plane leveled out. I looked over at the dials to see what our altitude was, but I couldn't decide which instrument would give me that information.

"What's our altitude?" I asked.

"Ten thousand feet," he said.

I nodded. "That's supposed to be best. High enough to make good headway, but not so high that you can't tell what's below."

He looked surprised.

"That's right," he said. "I'm a little surprised you know that."

"I know a little about a lot of things," I said, seeking to change the subject.

"You're a college professor, right?"

"Yes," I said. "I do some administrative work, too, but I'm a professor at heart."

I couldn't say why I was telling him this. It wasn't something I told people. As far as anyone knew, my family included, I liked working in administration. The promotion had come with a nice bump in salary, not to mention the prestige that came with the title.

Since my family valued success, I let them believe that I was happy to get the promotion. After all, who wouldn't be?

"I'm sorry to hear that," Bradford said. "I firmly believe that a person should pursue the career that makes them happiest."

I had an image of myself sitting in front of a blank canvas, picking up a brush, and carefully dabbing on that first brush of color.

From there a blank canvas could be anything.

And that was what I loved doing the most.

"I agree," I said. "I didn't say I didn't like doing it. I just…"

I just did it because it was expected.

But I had the next two months to spend in Whiskey Springs mentoring students who loved art as much as I did while implementing a pilot program for doing just that.

That would be satisfying and enjoyable.

Even if it meant spending time in a state I had never been to. Doing something I had never done.

Even if it wasn't painting, exactly, it was a challenge. A challenge was the next best thing to painting.

Bradford gave me a little nod and in that moment, I got the sense, whether it was right or wrong I couldn't say, that he understood me.

That in itself was quite an accomplishment.

There weren't too many people who seemed to understand me, and even fewer who actually did.

Chapter Six

Bradford

I found Charlotte to be a delightful passenger.

Not only was she beautiful, but she seemed to understand the basics of flying.

I found myself talking out loud as I made adjustments here and there. Reading information from the gauges aloud, also.

She hung on every word as though I was talking to her about something she might actually enjoy. Like maybe art at the Met.

"When you are being a college professor," I asked. "What do you teach?"

"Art," she said.

"Art. So you're an artist?" I looked over at her sideways. I couldn't say that she looked like an artist. A college professor, yes, I could see that, but I couldn't see the artist in her.

She didn't fit the stereotype of what I thought an artist might look like. I told her so.

"You don't look like an artist."

"And what does an artist look like?" she asked with an impish little smile.

I liked it.

What did an artist look like?

"I'm not sure," I said. "Maybe you should be wearing one of those apron things."

"A smock?"

"Yes. A smock."

"I have a smock that I wear when I'm painting," she said. "But I don't normally wear it when I go out in public. When I'm not painting."

"That makes sense," I said.

Sensible. She was sensible. I didn't think of artists as being sensible. Maybe it wasn't so much how they looked as it was how they acted.

Since I didn't want to risk insulting her, as that wasn't my intent whatsoever, I decided not to share that particular insight with her.

"How much further?" she asked. "Before we land?"

I glanced down.

"Approximately ninety minutes."

"Oh."

"Are you bored already?"

"No," It's not that," she said. "What do you do when you have to use the restroom?"

Ah. "There's a restroom in the back of the airplane. You're welcome to unbuckle and go use it."

"Now?"

"Sure. It's a smooth flight."

She immediately unhooked her harness and stood up.

"I'll be right back," she said, making her way out of the cockpit into the cabin.

I smiled as she left.

It was true that we had just met, but I felt like we had known each other for a long time and not only that.

I felt like we were kindred spirits.

My trip to Whiskey Springs had just gone from an excuse to fly to so much more. I wanted to know everything about Charlotte.

I wanted to know what she painted. I wanted to watch her paint.

Even more, I wanted to just be with her.

I didn't even care what we did.

I had to figure out just how I was going to make that happen.

Chapter Seven

CHARLOTTE

On my surprisingly smooth trip to the restroom, I found William sound asleep, his air pods in his ears.

I'd been nervous about this trip. And I couldn't say I'd been happy about it to begin and end it all.

It had so far, however, turned out to be much more pleasant that I had anticipated.

It had come as a surprise to learn that we were flying private. It truly didn't seem necessary. We could have flown commercial just as easily.

But... I was so glad we had flown private instead.

I was truly fascinated. I was getting a good feel for why the men in my family enjoyed flying so much.

We would be at our destination in no time. We hadn't had to go through security to get on the airplane. And we didn't have to land in Denver and drive to Whiskey Springs. According to everything I'd read, Whiskey Springs was about a two hour drive from Denver on winding mountainous roads.

We were going to just fly straight in to the Whiskey Springs airport. We'd be there just like that. No checked baggage. No hassle.

It wasn't just that, I admitted to myself as I made my way back to the cockpit. It was Bradford. My pilot. The trip was far more interesting having such a handsome pilot. He was friendly. Explained things as he did them. I didn't understand most of it, but it didn't matter. I liked hearing him explain things. He had a calm, confident voice. I could imagine that he would stay calm in the face of an emergency and keep others calm along with him. An admirable trait for a pilot to have.

I tried to picture my brothers in their roles as pilots, being confident and calm, but I couldn't quite do it.

Just like the uniform.

Bradford wore the pilot's uniform far better than my brothers. Of course, they were my brothers. It was natural, I suppose that I would find Bradford more handsome in his uniform than my brothers. But it wasn't just the uniform. It was everything.

I didn't date. First of all, I didn't date students. And second I didn't date people I worked with, faculty or staff.

Since most of my time was spent at work, that didn't leave a whole lot of options. I wasn't interested in dating apps. Not that I was against them. I just truly did not have the time or energy required.

My younger sister, an architect, had just gone into business for herself and she'd asked me to help her out by adding some interior design touches to what she called her office cottage designs. I was not an interior designer, but I had a good eye for color.

So not only was I an assistant administrator for the college, a professor, a consultant for my sister, and when time allowed, an artist. Not much room in there for dating even if I wanted to.

I was of the mind that things like that happened when they were supposed to happen.

I took my seat and this time I harnessed myself in.

"You're a quick study," Bradford said.

"So I've been told."

"I'm impressed."

I grinned with the compliment, small that it was.

"You want to take the controls?" he asked.

I felt my eyes widen.

"Now you're just teasing me," I said.

"Not something I would tease about."

"No," I said, shaking my head. "I'll leave the flying to the experts. Now if you want me to paint a new design on your dashboard, then we'll talk."

"Somehow I don't think Noah Worthington would be a big fan of that."

"No," I said. "I think you're right about that."

I would have to stick to painting canvases. Not that it was a hardship.

Nor was it a hardship sitting next to Bradford Torres.

Chapter Eight

BRADFORD

As I prepared for our initial descent I considered my conversation with Charlotte.

Most people in Houston knew who Noah Worthington was. In Pittsburgh, not so much.

But she didn't bat an eye. She knew who Noah Worthington was.

This girl continued to surprise me.

She might not have initially known how to buckle herself up or that there was a restroom in the back of the airplane, but she knew more about flying than she might admit.

She was most definitely a mystery.

"Prepare for initial descent," I said, for no particular reason.

"Won't be long now," I told Charlotte.

She nodded and straightened in her chair.

The Rocky Mountains were visible now. Breathtaking as always coming in from the east. It always made me think about the pioneers who had traveled west. Watching the mountains inch closer and closer day by day. It must have been a baffling thing for them to experience.

Checking the gauges, I prepared to give landing all my attention. The winds were different out here in the mountains.

When the runway came in sight, I flipped off the autopilot and lowered the wheels.

"It's so small," Charlotte said.

"It just looks small," I said. "But the airplane is smart enough to practically land itself."

"I doubt that," she said.

"I'll give it a little help," I said.

And I did just that. I took the airplane in for a smooth landing if I did have to say so myself.

"Nice landing," Charlotte said.

"Thanks." I didn't mention just how white her knuckles were. "You make a fine copilot," I said instead.

She beamed. "Thank you. I do what I can."

I taxied toward the little building that served as a terminal.

"Do you have someone picking you up?" I asked.

"I have no idea," she said, looking around. "I think maybe I should have checked into that."

"I think maybe that would have been a good idea. But I can take care of it."

"Okay," she said, turning on her phone.

She watched as I went through the post flight checklist.

"Think we should wake up your friend?"

"Graduate assistant," she clarified.

"Graduate assistant." That definitely made sense. Whatever it was she was coming out here to do, she had brought her grad assistant.

"Any idea how long you're staying?"

"They told me eight weeks," she said, looking into my eyes.

Eight weeks. She was here for eight weeks and I was here until further notice.

Perhaps there was a chance I could see more of Dr. Charlotte Ashton.

I turned on my phone to find a text from Maggie. Maggie was the office guru. She took care of everything. And in true form, she had a car on the way.

"A car will be here shortly," I said.

"That fast?"

"Compliments of Skye Travels."

She waited patiently while I went through the post flight checklist.

"Are you from Pittsburgh?" she asked.

"Houston," I said.

"You flew from Houston to Pittsburgh to Whiskey Springs in one day?"

"What? No. I flew up from Houston yesterday."

She nodded.

"Are you flying back to Houston now?"

"No," I said, turning to face her. "I'm staying in Whiskey Springs until further notice."

"Oh." She smiled, biting her lower lip and looking at me with her forest green eyes. Eyes that called to me like a siren's song, luring me onto the rocks.

What were the odds, I wondered, that I would be able to stay here for two months? Or even at least a few days?

Chapter Nine

Charlotte

Standing outside the airplane with William on one side and Bradford on the other, we waited for our ride to pick us up from the airport.

Almost time for lunch, the sun was warm on our heads and the breeze was cool. The scent of jet fuel mixed with what smelled like fresh blue spruce trees after a rain.

The aspen trees surrounding the runway had turned a lovely shade of yellow. The sound of their leaves lived up to their name—quaking aspens.

Mixed in with the aspens, here and there, were maple trees, their leaves turning a bright red.

The red and yellow leaves mixed with the green of the spruce trees created a lovely canvas of colors.

Mountain peaks wearing white caps of snow stood in the distance, high above the trees.

The airport was just a single runway with a little building, what served as the terminal, at one end. The building appeared to be closed and Bradford didn't take us there.

He had filled out all his paperwork on his iPad before we left the airplane.

"It's beautiful here," I said. The air felt clean and light. Although the mountain tops stretched high above us, we were still high in elevation.

"It is," Bradford said.

William had his head bent over his phone, typing a message, not even glancing up.

"Everything okay, William?" I asked. He had been my student. He knew how I felt about people being glued to their devices.

"Yes ma'am, Dr. Ashton." He slid his phone in his pocket.

A old diesel pickup truck turned into the parking lot and slowly approached us.

I paid little attention to it until it stopped next to the airplane. I looked over at Bradford questioningly. Surely this was not our ride.

Bradford went up to the man's open window and they spoke briefly.

He turned back to me.

"This is our ride," he announced.

William and I looked at each other.

He was jesting, of course. There was no way the four of us were going to fit in the cab of that pickup truck.

"I don't think so," I said, not realizing until it was too late that I said it out loud.

The driver stepped out and walked around the truck. He was wearing stiffly pressed blue jeans, black cowboy boots, and a flannel shirt, all topped off by a black cowboy hat.

"They didn't tell me there would be three of you," he said, chewing on gum or tobacco and hooking his thumbs in his back pockets.

"Didn't know when they made the reservation," Bradford said.

I pulled out my cell phone.

"It's okay," I said. "I'll just schedule an Uber. We can wait."

The driver and Bradford looked at each other.

"Sorry, ma'am," the driver said. "I'm the closest thing you're gonna get to an Uber around here."

I opened my app anyway and scowled at it. He was right. The closest Uber from here was in Boulder. It would take an hour at best for a driver to get here.

With a sigh, I put my phone away.

"He's right," I told William.

"How far is the walk?" William asked, looking toward the road.

"Too far," Bradford said, quickly dismissing that idea.

"You can take Bradford to town," I said. "We can wait for you to come back."

"Not a chance," Bradford said, opening the squeaking door to the truck. "William," he said. "You climb in the middle."

William did as he was told and the driver went around and climbed back in his seat.

I looked at the remaining space, then looked at Bradford.

"I have pretty good spatial skills," I said. "We're not very big, but there's no way we're going to fit."

"You might have good spatial skills," he said with a little smile. "But I'm better at physics."

Chapter Ten

BRADFORD

Ten minutes later, we were all in the old pickup truck and rumbling out toward the main road. The muffler was too loud and the truck didn't have air conditioning. Fortunately, he usually didn't need it.

I knew the driver. His name was Walter and he was one of Whiskey Spring's two unofficial Uber drivers.

Whiskey Springs didn't have an official Uber service.

He usually picked me up in his old truck and it wasn't a problem.

Today, however, he should have brought a car, assuming he had one.

I was not, however, complaining.

By not hesitating and doubtless throwing Charlotte off guard, I had her sitting in my lap.

We were no doubt breaking all sorts of laws and even those that just served as safety suggestions. Like a passenger riding in the middle of a pickup truck cab without a seatbelt. Probably a law. If not, it was at least a strong suggestion.

For good reason.

But Walter drove slowly and safely.

It wasn't William, though, that I was concerned about.

I had Charlotte sitting in my lap.

She was light as a feather and sat still as a statue.

"We can be fined," she said.

"They won't fine us," I said. "I know the sheriff."

Even though I couldn't see her, I *felt* her making a face.

As Walter made the turn onto the main highway, I had to wrap my arms around Charlotte to keep her from sliding off. She grabbed at the door, whether to hold on or jump out I couldn't be one hundred percent certain.

At any rate, with one hand braced against the door, she put her other hand over my arm.

In my opinion, this was much better. Now if she would just relax against me...

"Where am I taking you all?" Walter asked.

I nudged Charlotte, urging her to answer first.

"A saloon of some sort."

"The Whiskey Springs Saloon," Walter said. "Good choice."

"Wasn't my choice," I heard her mumble.

I had a feeling none of this, not even this trip was her idea.

"I'm staying there, too, Walter," I said. "One stop takes care of us."

"You're going to like the saloon, ma'am," he said.

I felt Charlotte cringe. I happened to know that a young lady often took offense at being called ma'am.

But Walter was an older fellow entrenched in his ways. He didn't mean anything by it.

"It's not bad," I whispered in her ear.

"Good to know," she said, with a little shiver.

This was interesting. She obviously didn't want to be sitting in my lap, but whispering in her ear caused her to shiver.

"Don't worry," I said, needing to test it out again. "I've got your back."

She raised her shoulder to her ear. I hadn't imagined it. I smiled to myself as Walter drove into downtown Whiskey Springs.

This was going to be an interesting stay. However long it happened to be.

Chapter Eleven

CHARLOTTE

The Whiskey Springs Saloon, I soon learned, was the very first building in the town. It was won in a bet in the early 1860s and soon got the reputation for having whiskey that never ran dry. Hence the name of the town: Whiskey Springs.

It went through a boom phase, but plateaued and never grew past being a small town.

It was known for Christmas. The town's slogan was "If Christmas was a town, it would be Whiskey Springs." Starting around Thanksgiving, everything that didn't move got decorated with lights or tinsel or ribbon or something Christmassy.

The festivities lasted all of December, but increased as Christmas neared.

The saloon itself was no longer a saloon, exactly, even though it embraced its heritage.

As we stepped inside, we were greeted by live piano music played by a girl dressed in a saloon girl costume—a long ruffled red dress, a little low at the bodice with underskirts with even more ruffles. She appeared to be having a really good time playing the piano. Her eyes were closed and her fingers swept over the keys.

The lunch crowd also seemed to be enjoying themselves sitting at tables. A couple of them had children with them. A family restaurant, despite its name.

It did, however, have a bar and a couple of people sat on the stools despite it being early in the day.

A large staircase led up to the second floor where a railing revealed the dozen or so doors to the rooms.

"Are you hungry?" Bradford asked.

"I am," William spoke up.

"I'll have our luggage sent up if you want to find a table," Bradford said, motioning for what appeared to be a bellhop to take our luggage.

Since we hadn't checked in yet, it didn't seem likely that the bellhop would know where to take our luggage, but apparently he did. Or if he didn't, he did a good job of faking it.

The three of us found a table near the window. Although the saloon was obviously old, the window looked surprisingly modern. A floor to ceiling window bringing in a perfect view of the snow-capped mountains.

A server, a young man dressed in formal black brought us menus and water.

"Can I start you off with a salad?" he asked.

"Sure," Bradford said.

Taking our cues from him, William and I nodded in agreement.

He left our menus, even though he seemed to already know what we wanted to order.

Bradford didn't open his menu.

"Are we supposed to look at these?" I asked, picking up one of the menus.

"Of course," he said. "I already know what I'm going to order."

"What do you recommend?" I asked.

"They have the best hamburger and fries in town. I always get that."

"I'll have that, too," William said.

After a quick glance at the menu, I closed it and set it aside. "Seems unanimous," I said.

"You have to eat your salad first, though," Bradford said with a straight face.

And right on cue, our server brought out our salads.

"Yes sir," he said. "The owner is giving away complimentary salads to promote healthy eating."

"I've never heard of anyone doing that before," I said.

"Whiskey Springs is not the usual town."

"Huh." I sat back and looked around. The customers seemed normal enough. Besides the two families with children, there were several couples and a group of older men sitting at one of the larger tables.

"Why do you say that?" I asked, turning back to Bradford.

"It's rife with legends about couples being reunited here over the years, especially in its early days. Some say it has a magical quality to it."

"Is that so? I can see why people would come here. It's charming."

"Once people move here, they don't usually leave." He took a swallow of water. "Unless they're from here."

"What does that mean?" I asked with a little laugh and a little bit of concern. I wasn't moving here, exactly, unless living here for two months counted.

"I think it's a universal thing, isn't it? Young people want to leave the place they grew up?"

"I never wanted to leave Pittsburgh," I said.

"I guess then you're the anomaly."

"I guess so. Have you always lived in Houston?"

"Born and bred."

"You wanted to leave?"

"Not really," he said.

He was smiling, his blue eyes twinkling.

"I guess we're both anomalies, then," I said.

I didn't mind being an anomaly with Bradford. In fact, it made me feel a bit of a kinship with him.

Then I remembered that he was from Houston and I was from Pittsburgh.

That was particularly relevant since we both admittedly did not want to leave our hometowns.

"Can I take your order?" the server asked.

As we placed our orders, I decided that I had some thinking to do, but I could do that thinking later.

Right now was the time to enjoy the live old-fashioned piano music and the company of a handsome pilot.

It didn't even matter that we had a chaperone in the form of my graduate student.

Chapter Twelve

Bradford

I had always liked Whiskey Springs. As I had mentioned to Charlotte, I'd always heard that it had a magical aspect to it, but I had never felt it myself.

Until now.

Sitting here in the saloon, hundreds of years old, with Charlotte, I felt some of that magic.

Piano music swirled through the air, blending seamlessly with conversations and the click of silverware.

I had been to the Whiskey Springs Airport a few times since I'd gone to work for Noah Worthington. I'd even stayed overnight here at the saloon a couple of times. Noah kept a room on reserve at all times. No one ever really said what Noah's special affinity for Whiskey Springs was. Maybe he just liked it.

As Charlotte said, it was charming.

I had to admit that seeing it through her eyes, I saw its charm for the first time. Until tonight, it had simply been another destination.

I hadn't considered myself jaded. I was a pilot and would never consider doing anything else. I'd wanted to be a pilot since I was a boy and my grandfather took me to the Houston airport.

Grandpa had always wanted to fly airplanes. It had been his most fervent dream in life.

But he had died before he ever had the chance to follow through and live that dream.

He had never, in fact, flown in an airplane.

Maybe that was why I had become a pilot. Maybe I had been following his dream for him.

But somewhere along the way, his dream had become my dream.

Lately though, I realized now, I had been going through the motions.

Not just with flying, but with my life as well.

My dating life, especially. Like most pilots, I never had trouble finding companionship whether I was in Houston or traveling.

I'd never had a date in Whiskey Springs. Maybe the legend had made me wary. I couldn't really say.

But sitting here with Charlotte, I not only believed in the legend, I embraced it.

"What do you have planned for the day?" I asked her as we finished up our lunch.

She glanced over at William.

"William and I need to find the building that's going to serve as our classroom," she said.

"Where is it?" I asked.

"324 Main Street," she said without a hitch.

I was rather impressed that she knew that without looking it up.

I wanted to see her again. I wanted to take a walk around town with her.

But with William sitting here acting as our unintentional chaperone, I kept that to myself.

Since I was going to be here for awhile, I'd find another way to go about it.

"Well," I said. "I'll go and see if I can get our keys."

"Don't we need to check in?" she asked.

"This is Whiskey Springs," I said as I stood up. "There's no need for formalities."

I left her there, sitting with William, and went in search of our keys.

In truth, I needed some distance. Some time to think and to remember why I was here.

Charlotte obviously had not forgotten why she was here.

I would do well to follow her lead.

Chapter Thirteen

CHARLOTTE

My hotel room was an interesting mix of old and new. The small room had a full-sized canopied bed with a crisp white comforter and curtains that matched on both the bedposts and the little window.

The bathroom was small, obviously added in long after the saloon had been built, with a little shower. But with obvious ingenuity, they had installed a clawfoot bathtub in the bedroom itself in a little alcove. Water ran through exposed pipes to a faucet on a pole, adding to its charm.

I was so impressed with that unique use of space that I photographed it and texted my sister the pictures. As an architect she would be impressed. Perhaps she could even use it for inspiration in one of her designs.

The view from the little window looked out toward the tall

rugged snowcapped mountain peaks on the other side of a meadow with a river running through it.

Perhaps I would explore later. Take a walk along the riverbank. Find a place for my students to spend some time painting.

The program, I had learned, was less of a classroom setting and more of an internship. The students who signed up would be spending their time painting landscapes. That was the purpose of choosing Whiskey Springs as the location.

This was an ideal place for students to explore their painting abilities with a mix of hands on experience and guidance. I would be providing the guidance while nature provided the landscape.

I looked forward to meeting the students who apparently had been carefully chosen from hundreds of applications from all over the country. I expected them to be some of the best of the best.

They all came highly recommended. I had their applications downloaded on my computer and had every intention of looking over them tonight if not today. I'd acquaint myself with them before I even met them.

Since we would be spending the better part of eight weeks together, it wouldn't hurt to get a head start on learning about them.

I opened the larger of my suitcases and began unpacking.

When it came right down to it, the person I really wanted to get to know was Bradford.

But once he had distributed our keys, he had vanished.

I'd thought perhaps I would see him again, but apparently riding in the cockpit, sitting in a man's lap in an old truck, and having lunch with him didn't mean to him what it meant to me.

I laid my favorite painter's smock on one of the shelves in the little cabinet that served as a closet and even that reminded me of Bradford.

I shook it off.

This is what happened when a girl didn't date.

I tried to remember the last time I'd gone on a date. It had been a double date with my younger sister. That was so long ago, it was before Bella was even reunited with her husband.

Neither one of us had had a good time that night. Both of our dates were questionable. That was the last time we had double-dated.

And it was the last time I had been on a date at all.

Spending time with Bradford, a charming, handsome pilot, was an overload for my senses.

From looking into his sparkling blue eyes to engaging conversation, I had been reminded what it was like to spend time in the company of a man other than my brothers, students, or colleagues.

I wasn't here to crush on my handsome pilot and certainly not to date. I was here to work.

So I tucked Bradford neatly into a back corner of my mind and gathered up what I needed to take with me down to what would be my office for the next eight weeks.

I had a job to do.

Chapter Fourteen

Bradford

I stood at the edge of the Whiskey Springs River and watched the rushing water tumbling over the boulders scattered through it.

Somehow the water found its way around boulders bigger than a small car. No stopping it, the water went where it pleased.

A couple of chipmunks raced up and stood on their hind legs at my feet, then just as quickly rushed off again. Feeding them was against the rules in most places and I had no reason to think it would be any different here.

The rugged, majestically tall mountains were so close, it almost looked like I could just cross the wooden foot bridge and walk right over to them.

Snow capped at the peaks, like ice cream cones dipped in white chocolate, they were bright with yellow, gold, red, and orange leaves down their sides.

In truth, though, I knew that they weren't actually that close. It was one of those deceptions of distance that happened in the mountains.

It was quite a change from the flat landscape of Houston that I was accustomed to. I could certainly get used to it.

If I was an artist, this is a place I would want to capture on a canvas.

Maybe I would bring Charlotte here to the riverbank. As an artist, she would appreciate it. Maybe she would even want to paint it. It was definitely worth painting.

My attempt at not thinking about her wasn't going so well.

While I had been thinking about how I could get her away from her graduate assistant and explore the town today, she had been thinking about and planning on going to work.

It was what she was here for. I understood that. I was here for work, as well.

I guess I thought that since I was enchanted by her, that she would be enchanted with me as well.

Maybe I had been hopeful.

Since I didn't have cell phone service out here, I decided to head back along the path toward town.

It was a peaceful walk beneath the colorful yellow-leaved aspen trees and red leaves falling from the maple trees.

I finally understood why people made a big deal out of coming out to see the changing colors of the leaves.

It truly was a breathtaking phenomenon of nature.

And from what I understood, it wouldn't be long before the snow started falling.

I would make it a point to come back, maybe at Christmas. I was curious to see if it really was everything they said it was.

If Christmas was a town, it would be Whiskey Springs was a bold claim that shouldn't be made lightly.

I was curious to see it for myself.

As I neared Main Street, I found myself doing some math. Charlotte would be back in Pittsburgh by then. If I wanted to bring her with me, I would have to swing by Pittsburgh and pick her up. Not a hardship.

There was one problem though. There was quite a bit of work to be done between where I stood right now with her and where I needed to be in order to bring her with me to Whiskey Springs in December.

My resolve to leave her be and let her focus on work was crumbling at a rate faster than the rapids tumbling over the boulders in the river.

I especially knew I was in trouble when I found myself searching for 324 Main Street.

I got back to the Whiskey Springs Hotel without finding it.

Disappointed, I went to the bar and climbed onto a bar stool. Since I was technically on call, meaning that if the Skye Travels office called me to take a flight, I couldn't have a drink, so I ordered a citrus spritzer and entertained myself by listening to the piano music and watching people come and go.

After about three minutes of that, I realized I was looking for Charlotte.

No point in fighting it.

I got on my phone and used my GPS to find 324 Main Street.

Chapter Fifteen

CHARLOTTE

Our temporary office space wasn't very big, but it was big enough. A dozen students and their canvases would fit in here easily.

Not that I planned on keeping them inside for long. The whole point of being in this picturesque little town was so that they could flex their muscles at painting landscapes. Of course, I had to plan on bad weather and we needed a place to store our supplies.

Bad weather was sure to keep us inside at least some of the time.

Whoever set up this internship should have consulted me first. I would have recommended summer. I'd never even been here, but even my quick Internet search warned me that the weather could turn temperamental this time of year.

But I would work with what we had. Whoever had picked this time of year had probably been thinking about the fall foliage.

The colorful foliage more than made up for any potential bad weather that I might concern myself with.

Whoever had rented the office space had thought to put in a little desk and desk chair that was perfect for computer work.

I had William unpacking boxes that had been delivered ahead of time and getting the canvases set up while I pulled up the student applications on my computer and began reviewing them.

Six female college students and six male college students. That was interesting. I wondered if it was intentional.

All of them were juniors majoring in art and all them came highly recommended by their professors.

Sitting back in the desk chair, I wondered how I had been chosen. I hadn't applied. In fact, if Dr. Jones had recommended me, he hadn't said anything to me about it.

"All unpacked and organized," William said, standing up and dusting his hands.

"Great," I said, looking over at William's neatly organized supplies. He was a good choice for my graduate assistant. I was lucky to have him here.

"Do you have anything else I need to do?" he asked, glancing over his shoulder toward the window at the people walking past.

"No," I said. "You did an awesome job. Why don't you take the rest of the day off? Do some exploring?"

"Okay," he said, smiling broadly. "Thank you."

As he left, I reminded myself that not everyone was as committed to work as much as I was. I had to remember that. William was a graduate student and needed time off.

Truth be known, I didn't mind having some time to myself.

I went back to my computer, making some notes on a legal pad as I went. It appeared the new students were all at about the same level and their applications included a sample of their work. Quite impressive work overall.

It would have been nice to have been in on the ground floor of this project. I would have enjoyed being part of the selection process. But if I was an applicant myself, that explained a lot.

When the door opened, I looked up, startled. I hadn't thought to lock the door after William left.

But it wasn't a stranger coming in through the door. It was Bradford.

"Hi," he said.

"Hi." I sat back in my chair and reflexively lowered the lid of my computer.

"Do you get time off?" he asked.

"I guess." I had just reminded myself that William needed time off. I hadn't even considered that for myself.

He smiled and I smiled back. It was his eyes that tugged at me. He seemed to be able to see deep into my soul. He actually *saw* me for who I was.

Chapter Sixteen

BRADFORD

Stepping out onto the sidewalk behind Charlotte and waiting for her to lock up the office, my mind raced with possibilities.

"Can I ask you a personal question?" I asked.

"Maybe." She straightened and looked at me. "What is it?"

"Did you bring any other shoes?"

She smiled, that smile that lit up her entire face.

"Yes," she said. "But..." She bit her lower lip. "I didn't bring any boots."

"Then we shall have to get you some."

"Oh. No. I don't—"

"I want to show you something," I said. "But you can't wear heels."

She looked up the street one way and down the street the other.

"There is no Nordstrom's here," she said.

I laughed.

"No," I said. "But there is a General Store." I nodded across the street.

"You think they have boots?"

"I think we should go and see."

"Okay," she said after a moment's hesitation.

"May I carry your book bag?" I asked.

"Okay." She lifted the leather satchel off her shoulders and handed it over to me. I didn't miss the little hint of relief that crossed her features.

I felt like a schoolboy carrying the girl's books to class.

Except instead of walking her to class, I was getting her to play hooky.

The general store had a little bit of everything.

Rows of food, boxes of macaroni and cheese, loaves of bread, potato chips, anything a person might want.

Souvenirs. T-shirts. Mugs. Scenic calendars.

And clothing. The back row was lined with hiking boots.

"I think they might be prepared," she said.

"I think you might be right. What size do you wear?"

"Six," she said, walking along, looking at the boots.

"See anything you like?"

"These," she said, picking up a pair of sturdy, but fashionable hiking boots, with lots of laces.

"Here's a size six," I said, pulling a box off the shelf. "Try them on?"

Sitting on a bench, she pulled one of the boots out of the boxes.

"I don't have socks."

"Not a problem," I said, grabbing a pair of decent looking socks off the rack.

Slipping out of her heels, she pulled on the socks.

"Can I help?" I asked, sliding to the floor in front of her.

"I can do it," she said, but straightened and put her hands on either side of her on the bench.

Hiding a smile, I began methodically lacing her boots.

"How does that feel?" I asked, looking up at her after I finished lacing one of her boots. "Is it a good fit?"

"Yes," she said. "Perfect."

She sat quietly while I laced up the other one.

"There you go," I said.

"You think I can wear them out?" she asked, looking over her shoulder.

"I don't see why not." I packed her heels in the boot box. I recognized them as designer heels, nonetheless.

It seemed a bit unlikely that a college professor would be wearing designer heels.

When we got to the checkout counter, I handed the clerk my credit card along with the box and the tag from the socks.

When Charlotte reached for her purse, I put a hand over hers.

"I got it," I said, leaning over to whisper in her ear.

"You shouldn't," she said.

"It was my idea," I said.

She just looked at me, looking a little baffled and amused at the same time.

"You're spoiling me," she said as I held the door open for her as we left the General Store.

"Then I'm doing something right," I said.

I considered dropping her satchel and shopping bag off at her room at the saloon, but decided against it. I didn't want to let her out of my sight for even a minute.

Chapter Seventeen

CHARLOTTE

Wearing my new boots, walking alongside Bradford, I admired the brightly colored yellow and red leaves on the trees along the trail. I easily navigated the firmly packed dirt trail littered with pebbles.

Already I could hear the rushing river up ahead.

Bradford assured me it was worth the hike, but I was enjoying the trail in and of itself. The colors begged to be painted on canvas.

I could set an easel up anywhere along this trail and be quite content.

Bradford, however, assured me that the river was even more picturesque, though I couldn't imagine how.

"How do your boots feel?" he asked.

"Quite comfortable. I would not want to walk this trail in heels."

"Not much further," he said, although I hadn't asked.

A little later, we reached the riverbank and he was right.

It was beautiful here. The snowcapped mountains provided a backdrop for the river and a meadow beyond it. The trees were even more colorful here or maybe there were just more of them. I'd never seen so many colorful trees in one place.

The sound of the quaking aspens was muffled by the roar of the rushing river. It wasn't very wide. Nothing like the Alleghany or the Ohio or the Monongahela.

The clear water sparkled in the sunlight.

When we reached a boulder on the side of the river, Bradford held out a hand.

I put my hand in his and he helped me balance as we climbed up on top of the rock.

The view was even better from up here.

As we stood there on the boulder, looking across the rushing river, I tried to figure out how I was going to get up here with a canvas. Perhaps I would just bring a sketchbook.

"What do you think?" he asked.

"I'm thinking I want to paint this."

"I thought you might."

He pulled his phone out of his pocket and snapped a few pictures.

"Selfie?" he asked.

"Sure," I said.

He put one arm around me, pulling me close, and took a photo of us with his other. I'd never mastered the art of holding a phone in one hand while taking a photo. Photography required two hands for me.

"I'll drop it to you," he said, proceeding to do so.

My phone chimed and I opened up the three pictures he had taken of us standing in front of the breathtaking view behind us.

I had to admit, we looked good together. And not only that, but I was surprised at the smile on my own face.

I looked happy. Happier than I had looked in a really long time.

Looking over at Bradford, my eyes misted.

"Are you okay?" he asked.

"It's the wind," I said. "I guess it burns my eyes."

"That happens sometimes," he said. "I should get you out of the wind."

He took my hand and together we climbed off the Boulder.

"When do your students start arriving?" he asked as we walked back down the trail toward town.

"Tomorrow," I said. "Some of them might already be here. I don't know. But classes start the next day. Day after tomorrow."

"How did you get chosen for this?"

"I honestly have no idea," I said. "I guess it was just one of those things I fell into."

"Well," he said. "I'm glad you did."

As was I. The fates had most definitely smiled down upon me.

I got more than I expected on this trip.

Chapter Eighteen

BRADFORD

It was the magic of Whiskey Springs, I decided as I walked back along the trail along with Charlotte.

That and fate.

There had to be some kind of magic involved for us to meet.

I hadn't originally even been scheduled for this trip.

It had originally been one of Noah's grandsons, but he had come down with a stomach virus at the last minute.

I just happened to be next on the list and available.

So Charlotte didn't know how she'd been chosen for this job that brought her to Whiskey Springs and I had been chosen by chance.

I didn't intend to let it slide past. To just be one of those insignificant encounters that quickly became no more than a memory.

"Can I take you to dinner?" I asked before I had time to overthink it.

"Where does one go to dinner in Whiskey Springs?"

"I don't know," I said. "But I will find out."

"There's always the saloon," she said.

"Yes," I said. "But that seems more like a lunch kind of place."

"You're thinking something more formal?" she asked. "Trying to get me back in my heels?"

"You read me like a book," he said.

"Okay. You figure out where and I'll wear my heels."

"I won't let you down," I said.

"I know," she said.

We walked in silence for the rest of the way to the saloon.

A saloon girl, a different girl, but also in a red dress, was playing the piano with as much gusto as the other girl at lunch.

Going up the wide stairway, I walked Charlotte to her hotel room door.

"I'll see you at six o'clock?" I asked.

She raised a brow.

"I know. Six o'clock is early, but it's eight on your time. Seven on mine. And besides, I don't know how long we'll have to wait for a table."

What I really meant was how far we'd have to travel.

"Six o'clock then," she said. "I'll see you then."

After I handed her the computer bag and shopping bag, she went inside and closed the door.

I stood there a minute, wondering how I got so lucky. Then I turned around walked next door to my own room.

I didn't know what had become of William, but he was a college student. He could take care of himself.

As for me, I had some research to do and some plans to make.

Tonight I had a date with the prettiest girl I had ever seen. And I had seen a lot of girls.

Sitting on the side of the bed, I started with google.

It didn't take but a few minutes before I called Maggie.

Maggie didn't have to be here to work her magic.

And tonight I wanted everything to be perfect.

Tonight I had a date with my dream girl.

Chapter Nineteen

CHARLOTTE

> ZOE
> Did you make it okay?

I sat on the side of the canopied bed and answered my best friend's text message.

> Safe and sound.

> ZOE
> How was the flight?

I laid back on the soft bed and settled in to text her back.

> My first flight ever was…

What was it anyway? Wonderful? Spectacular? Educational?

> Fun.

ZOE
Fun? Wait? Your first flight?

> Yep. My first time in the air.

While I waited for Zoe to answer, I checked the weather for Whiskey Springs tonight. Cool, but not cold. Pleasantly cool.

ZOE
How did that happen?

> I don't know.

ZOE
But... Henry and James. And Daniel.

I laughed as she named off the pilots in my family. My two brothers and my brother-in-law.

I silently added Bradford. My pilot as of today.

> I know. Somehow I just never went flying.

Thought bubbles.

ZOE
How was it fun?

> I sat in front. In the cockpit.

ZOE
Good for you.

I got up went to grab a bottle of water from my bag and stood at the window, looking out at the mountains in the distance. White clouds were clustered around them, hiding the peaks from view.

> ZOE
> You must be tired. Going to bed early tonight?

A couple of elk walked right out from the trees. Right out on the back lawn like they didn't have a care in the world.

> No. I have plans.

> ZOE
> Going through the applications?

I smiled to myself. How much did I want to tell Zoe? The problem was I just couldn't help myself. I had to tell her something.

> I'm going to dinner. Should I wear my green dress or my black dress?

> ZOE
> Green. It brings out your eyes.

> That's what I was going with.

I went to the closet and pulled my green dress from the cabinet that served as a closet. Laid it across the bed. Then I turned on the water to run a bath.

As I admired the freestanding faucet next to the clawfoot tub—so charmingly Victorian—Zoe wrote back.

> **ZOE**
> Wait. Is this a date?

> I think it is. I have to go get ready.

This was going to drive Zoe crazy. She lived for details. Especially with me since I hadn't dated in so long, certainly not due to a lack of her trying to fix me up.

Putting my phone on charge, I climbed into the steamy bath water.

It was a date and I was going to primp appropriately.

I had three texts from Zoe when I got out of the tub.

> **ZOE**
> Who?

> **ZOE**
> Who is your date with?

> **ZOE**
> You met someone out there already?

> Gotta run. I'll tell you later.

I had to dry and straighten my hair. I really didn't have time to chat.

I was going to take extra care in getting ready for my first date in years.

Chapter Twenty

BRADFORD

Since my room was right next to Charlotte's, it didn't seem fair to say that I was early when I went downstairs at five thirty.

I paced to the front door and back. The lively piano music had people talking louder and if I wasn't mistaken the girl at the piano only played that much louder, creating a reciprocally increasing loudness.

The saloon was crowded and all the stools at the bar were taken. I'd been right when I'd decided we should go somewhere else for dinner. Unfortunately Whiskey Springs didn't have any place that I considered nice enough for a real date. The only place in town considered better than this was the Hungry Biscuit.

According to their website, the Hungry Biscuit had white tablecloths and candles, but their specialty was burgers and fries just like the saloon.

I wondered if maybe someone was missing out by not putting in a fancy restaurant here in town. Maybe there just wasn't enough business for it all year round. They had busy seasons like December and summer.

So I made other arrangements.

On my third trip to the front door, I turned around and started toward the stairs again.

About halfway across the room, I missed a step and stopped.

Charlotte stood there at the top of the stairs.

She wore a slim body-hugging sparkling green dress. It skimmed the floor, revealing a peek of her heels when she lifted her skirts before starting down the stairs.

Seeing me standing here, she smiled at me.

I forced myself to breathe. She'd done something with her hair. Straight with little curls on the ends, it swirled around her shoulders. Loads of beautiful brunette hair.

The big grandfather clock standing at the bottom of the stairs began to chime the hour. It chimed six times by the time Charlotte reached the bottom step where she stopped.

Unable to keep my hands off of her, I put my hands on her waist and lifted her off her feet.

She gasped and put her hands on my shoulders.

Twirling her around before setting her on her feet, I kissed her on the forehead.

"You're beautiful," I said. The green of her sparkling dress made her green eyes sparkle all the more.

"You were right," she said. "We're a little overdressed for the saloon."

Taking her arm, I tucked it in the crook of my arm and led her toward the door.

"People are looking at us," she said, leaning close.

"How could they not?" I said. "You're the most beautiful woman in the town."

She rolled her eyes, but I didn't miss the little flush of color that spread across her cheeks.

We stepped outside.

"I think we should have brought a sweater," she said with a little shiver.

"It's all taken care of," I said steering her toward a car. A real car. Not an old pickup truck.

I opened the back door and held it open for her.

"This is our car?" she asked.

"Not as comfortable as the truck, but it'll do," I said.

She smiled as she climbed inside the car and I climbed in beside her.

"Evening, Sir," the driver said.

"Good evening Reginald."

"Any change in plans?"

"None," I said, taking Charlotte's hand.

"Do I get to know where we're going?" she asked me, keeping her voice low.

"Are you one of those women who don't like surprises?" I asked, with a little smile.

"I don't mind," she said. "As long as it's a good surprise."

"I think you'll like it. But I won't tell you because it'll ruin the surprise."

Smiling, she leaned toward the middle and looked out the window to see which direction we were going.

"We're going to the airport," she said.

"It's hard to surprise a college professor," I said with mock disappointment.

She just shrugged.

"Is there a restaurant out this way?"

"Something like that."

"Hmm. Not on Google," she said.

So she had been on the Internet, too. Nothing got past her.

"You'll see," I said, taking her hand.

When her phone chimed, she pulled it out of her little handbag to read the text. It crossed my mind that it was curious that she brought formal evening clothes to Whiskey Springs.

"Everything okay?" I asked.

"It's my best friend Zoe. She's worried about me."

"Why would she be worried?"

"I rather left things to the imagination."

"Like what?"

"Like... she's afraid you might be a serial killer."

"Never been accused of that one before," I said, wryly.

She shrugged and turned her phone over.

"She'll wait."

I liked this girl more and more. Like me, she seemed to prefer to keep some things to herself.

Chapter Twenty-One

CHARLOTTE

I wasn't surprised when the driver turned into the airport parking lot and stopped next to the airplane.

I did, after all, have three pilots in the family. Just because I had never experienced some of what they did firsthand, I had heard the stories.

Bradford, though, seemed quite pleased with himself.

It didn't seem to bother him that we had just flown in earlier in the day.

That wasn't a surprise either. My brothers used any excuse they could find to go into the air, especially before they got married. Maybe now not quite so much.

By six thirty we were ready for takeoff. Just one of the many benefits of flying private.

No lines. No wait.

I got another text from Zoe.

> **ZOE**
> At least give me a name or send me a picture. Just in case he turns out to be a serial killer.

> I'll text you when I'm home safe.

Then we were airborne.

This was actually the first time I could ever remember being somewhere that no one knew where to find me.

I'd always been the safe one. The compliant one. I never complained about the rules. All I wanted to do was paint anyway.

It was a strange feeling, being in the air with Bradford. And no one knew it. Not even my best friend. Not even my sister. One or the other of them had always known where to find me.

"What are you thinking?" Bradford said, talking to me through the headphones.

"I'm thinking that I can see the allure of flying."

"You'd never flown before today."

I couldn't tell if he was asking me or making statement. So I didn't answer.

Instead, I pressed my forehead to the window and watched the lights of Whiskey Springs disappear behind us as the sun began its drop behind the mountains.

"Where are we going?" I asked.

"There's a little Italian restaurant in Boulder that sounded nice. Not that I've ever been there."

"Boulder," I said.

"We'll be there in no time."

I relaxed back against the seat. I really could get used to flying. Maybe it was in the Ashton blood. I'd heard people say that before, but I'd never paid much attention to it.

I'd like to paint from the sky, but of course, I didn't think I could do that. Maybe from a photograph. Or maybe from my memory.

Right now I just wanted to enjoy my date.

As far as first dates went, they didn't get much better than this.

I was glad I had packed a couple of my evening gowns. I hadn't even given it much thought. I'd just tossed them in. My sister always took nice clothes when she traveled, so I guess I had unconsciously picked it up from her.

True to his word, Bradford took us in for a landing in no time.

The Boulder airport was bigger than the Whiskey Springs airport. Of course, anything would have been.

There was a chauffeured car waiting for us there, too. For some reason, I found that impressive. More so than the car in Whiskey Springs and even more impressive than the airplane itself.

As we stepped off the airplane and got into the back seat of the car, I wondered if this was what it felt like to be royalty.

Bradford held my hand all the way out to the restaurant.

Maybe he was what made me feel like royalty.

It really had nothing to do with the airplane and the chauffeured cars.

It had everything to do with Bradford.

Chapter Twenty-Two

BRADFORD

It was dark by the time we got into the chauffeured car at the Boulder airport and began our ride to the restaurant.

I didn't normally go to so much trouble on my dates.

I should have noticed that, but somehow I hadn't. I hadn't been self-aware enough to notice that about myself.

But with Charlotte, everything was different. With Charlotte, I wanted to show her the world.

It didn't matter that I'd already flown halfway across the country once today. Another little flight to take her to a nice restaurant was nothing.

Sight unseen, I hoped it was nice enough. She was dressed so elegantly and looked even more like an elfin princess.

"Are you tired?" I asked.

"No." She shook her head. "This is much better than what I had planned."

"And what was that?"

"I'd probably have looked over some of the student records again or maybe would have read a novel I'm halfway through."

"What are you reading?"

"It's called a romantasy. I don't remember the title."

"Those are my sister's favorites," I said.

"You have a sister?"

"I actually have two of them," I said as we pulled up in front of the restaurant.

The chauffeur came around and opened the door.

I stepped out and was immediately pleased.

The little restaurant was set back in the trees, just like in the pictures. The walkway was lit with little white lights—an added touch not in the photos.

Another couple, dressed much as we were, came out the door as we were going in.

"This was a good choice," Charlotte said. "I'm impressed."

"Then so am I," I said as we reached the hostess desk. "We have a reservation for two. Bradford Torres."

"Yes, sir," the young lady said, "Would you and your wife please follow me?"

I felt the hesitation as I took Charlotte's hand to follow the hostess to our table, but I didn't correct her. I couldn't imagine what good that would serve.

Besides, I rather liked the idea.

I held her chair as she sat down, then sat across from her.

The hostess handed us menus before she walked off.

I set mine aside.

"You already know what you're going to order," she said.

"I admit to looking ahead."

"Well," she said, leaning back in her chair and opening her menu. "I'm going to look anyway."

"Okay," I said.

"It's expected," she said, looking at me over the menu.

"I don't mind." I raised my hands. "Honest."

I caught the glimpse of a smile before she raised the menu to hide her face.

Well. This was no good. This was not good at all. She was way over there on the other side of the table.

I got up and moved to the chair next to her, then grabbed my silverware and water glass.

She looked at me over the top of her menu, amusement in her eyes.

She was most definitely a siren. A siren masquerading as an artist and college professor.

"See anything you like?" I asked.

"Not yet," she said.

"Want some help?"

She shifted in her chair, then lowered the menu, placing it on the table between us.

"Since you won't open yours," she said. "We can share one."

"Sharing is good," I said. "I like sharing."

One of the servers brought us a basket of bread and filled our water glasses.

Drinking deeply from her water glass, she looked at me over the rim of her glass.

"You're trouble," she said.

"Me?" I sat back and grinned. "I think there's a compliment in there somewhere."

"I think maybe I should send Zoe a text with your name. Maybe your picture," she said before turning her attention back to her menu.

Charlotte Ashton was going to be fun.

Not just breathtakingly beautiful, but fun.

That was hard to find.

Chapter Twenty-Three

CHARLOTTE

After dinner, our car was waiting at the door. I hadn't even seen Bradford call for it, but somehow he must have. A text message perhaps.

"Thanks for waiting for us," Bradford told the driver.

"Not a problem. Straight to the airport?"

"Please."

With just street lights making a dent in the darkness, the driver hopped on the Interstate and headed toward the airport.

Bradford put an arm around me and pulled me against him.

"Are you tired?" I asked him the same thing he'd ask me earlier.

"Not even a little."

"Flying energizes you?"

"Actually yes. Good observation. By the way, how do you know so much about flying? And you say you haven't flown private before."

"I pay attention," I said, feigning sleepiness. I wasn't ready to tell him who I was yet and quite frankly I was surprised he hadn't figured it out.

"I guess you would," he said, kissing me on the top of my head.

I closed my eyes and breathed in his male scent. He smelled like spruce trees after a rain with a hint of jet fuel.

Not only did he smell good, but he felt good. It felt good to rest against him. Maybe a little too good.

It was odd because I didn't date. I didn't date coworkers or students and if anyone had asked me before today, I probably would have said that I didn't date pilots.

I had no real reason to feel that way. Except that I had two brothers who were pilots. I knew the kind of reputation that pilots had. In general.

I looked up at Bradford out of the corner of my eye. Was Bradford like that?

Was I just another one of his girls? Maybe his Whiskey Springs girl?

Temporary Whiskey Springs girl.

Had to be temporary because I was going back to Pittsburgh at the end of the two months.

Maybe he was thinking I would be his Pittsburgh girl at that point.

"What are you thinking about?" he asked.

"Not thinking."

"Okay," he said.

"Do you like flying at night?" I asked, steering him away from my real thoughts.

"I don't mind. I like flying any time. Day or night."

"You sound like my brothers," I said, then realized what I had said.

I had just blown my cover.

He pulled back a bit and looked down at me.

"Brothers?"

"I have three of them," I said. "And one sister."

"How many of your brothers are pilots?"

"Two. And one brother-in-law." I sighed.

"You didn't think I might find that relevant?"

"I didn't think about it at all."

"We have arrived at the airport," the driver announced as he stopped next to the airplane.

Bradford opened the door and held out a hand to assist me out.

Such a gentleman.

He was not only handsome and smart. And fun. He was a gentleman.

I was smitten with him.

I was smitten with a man I hardly knew.

Chapter Twenty-Four

BRADFORD

As I went through the preflight checklist with Charlotte sitting in the copilot's seat, my thoughts kept straying to her.

To her big green eyes that called to me like a siren calling to the sailors over the rocks.

To the way she felt when I'd held her close against me. So right. She had felt so right.

She watched everything I did. She had pilots in her family and she had never been up in a private plane. That was too baffling for me to even begin to understand.

I had taken both of my sisters up and I'd taken my parents up, too.

They had wanted to share in that part of my life and I had wanted to show off.

Charlotte came from a large family. One sister and three brothers. Five of them altogether.

But a big family was no excuse for her to be ignored. For her brothers to neglect taking her flying.

I didn't understand it, but it wasn't my place to do so.

What I could do was to do my part to make up for it.

I could take her flying and take her flying often.

I'd take her flying whenever she wanted to. Wherever she wanted to go.

But I was getting ahead of myself.

I taxied out onto the runway and waited for clearance to takeoff.

She was looking straight ahead now, so I studied her profile without her knowing. Studied her delicate elfin features.

I wanted to kiss her.

I was going to kiss her.

I just had to figure out when I was going to do it.

Charlotte wasn't the kind of girl a man just kissed for no reason.

I had a reason. I wanted to date her.

But there was a catch. Before I could kiss her, I had to let her know I wanted to date her.

I had let her know my intentions.

This was different from the way I had been rolling lately. Lately I had not been worrying about intentions because the truth was, I couldn't remember the last time I'd had honorable intentions.

It wasn't that I was a rogue. I was actually a nice guy. I had simply lost my way around girls lately.

Charlotte was the solution to that. Charlotte was the one who was going to save me from a life of wayward intentions.

She noticed me looking at her and turned to face me.

"What are you thinking about?" she asked.

"Want to have lunch tomorrow?"

"Tomorrow?"

"I know. We're still on our date tonight. But..." I looked into her eyes and knew what it was like to fall head over heels. Just like that.

"I don't want to miss making sure I see you again."

She smiled that little secret smile that women smiled when they knew they had a man in the palm of their hand.

"Okay," she said. "I'll have lunch with you."

I smiled.

"I—"

"Cleared for takeoff."

The voice from the control tower came through my headphones loud and clear. It couldn't have come at a worse time.

I'd been just about to tell her that I wanted to kiss her.

"Ready?" I asked.

She nodded.

"What were you going to tell me?"

"I..."

She was looking at me with such bafflement and anticipation that I decided to forego my own rules.

I leaned over close enough that my breath mingled with hers.

"I was going to tell you," I said. "that I would like to kiss you."

"Now?" she asked, her voice no more than a whisper.

"Now seems like a good time."

She swallowed and just looked at me. She didn't move.

I leaned forward a little more and lightly pressed my lips against hers.

But it wasn't enough.

It wasn't nearly enough.

I deepened the kiss and she kissed me back.

"Cleared for takeoff."

I pulled back with a groan.

"I think we have to go now."

"Okay," she breathed, nodding.

I nodded, too. "We have to go now."

"Okay."

"Okay."

Chapter Twenty-Five

CHARLOTTE

> His name is Bradford.

I lay across my bed and prepared to be interrogated by Zoe. She wasted no time writing back.

> ZOE
> I guess he's not a serial killer.

> He's a pilot.

> ZOE
> Oh boy.

Piano music drifted up the stairs and into my room. The girl playing at the moment wasn't as skilled as the other girls I'd heard playing throughout the day. I wondered just how late into the night they would play. Either way, I didn't think it would disturb my sleep.

> I think something's wrong with me.

ZOE
Why? What happened?

> I think I'm crushing on him and I just met him.

> Today.

Thought bubbles.
Then nothing.
I got up and changed out of my dress.

ZOE
I think that's how it works. I wouldn't be worried.

I set my heels in the cabinet.

> I don't think it's smart.

ZOE
LOL

> What's funny?

ZOE
You are so long overdue.

I hung up my dress and smoothed it out. Pulled on a t-shirt.

> Overdue for what?

> **ZOE**
> When is the last time you even had a date?

> I don't know.

> **ZOE**
> Get some sleep. Have some good dreams.

> Seriously? That's your answer.

> **ZOE**
> Good night Charlotte.

Some friend she was. No sympathy whatsoever for my plight.

I had to admit, though, that she was right. I needed to stop worrying and just get some sleep.

Tomorrow I had to work. Tomorrow I would start meeting my students.

And that, I reminded myself, was the reason I was here.

I was not in Whiskey Springs to go on dates with handsome pilots.

Still. That was a nice side benefit.

No one said I couldn't date while I was here.

There were no rules against that.

And if there were, I was going to happily break them.

Tomorrow Bradford was taking me to lunch. Something about a hungry biscuit.

I would look it up tomorrow. I yawned.

Tonight, though, I had some other things to look up.

And one of them was Bradford Torres.

I knew for a fact that Skye Travels had little bios on their website about their employees.

It wouldn't be anything too personal.

But right now I wanted to know every detail I could find about him.

Chapter Twenty-Six

BRADFORD

Up early the next day, I found a coffee shop on Main Street that sold designer coffees that rivaled anything I could find in Houston.

Coffee in hand, I took what was now my favorite trail down to the river. I sat on the larger boulder and watched the water swirling as it passed below.

A trout somehow swam against the current. I couldn't begin to imagine how. It seemed like it would take extraordinarily strong muscles.

Did fish have muscles?

I would look it up later. Maybe.

Right now I watched the sun slowly brightening the skies over the tops of the mountains before making its appearance.

It was my favorite time of day. Everything had a clean and fresh feel to it.

And the day held unspoken promises that anything was possible.

A city boy at heart, I was accustomed to watching the sun rise over tall buildings while traffic slowly picked up.

I often watched the sunrise from the balcony of my thirty-fifth floor one bedroom apartment in downtown Houston. My homemade coffee was not nearly as good as this coffee though.

And. I had never, not once, seen three elk walk out from the cover of the trees to drink from the river.

I sat very still, not wanting to scare away the elk.

Moving very slowly, I pulled out my phone and snapped a photo of them.

I'd show it to Charlotte. Maybe it would motivate her to want to come out here and watch the sunrise with me.

But there I was getting ahead of myself again.

We'd had dinner and today we were having lunch.

Things were going along quite well.

And that kiss...

I couldn't stop thinking about that kiss.

I'd kissed her again outside her door at the saloon, but it had been a simple, chaste kiss.

I wanted to pace myself. I wanted to do things right with Charlotte.

As the elk wandered back into the trees, I asked myself what doing things right meant to me.

Maybe I was being idealistic. Putting her on a pedestal.

There was nothing wrong with that.

My older sister's husband put her on a pedestal and they had a happy marriage. Very happy from all accounts. He would do anything for her.

They had gotten married when they were eighteen. I'd been sixteen at the time of the wedding. My sister and her husband had always set the bar for what I wanted in a marriage.

It was probably why I had never been satisfied with any of my relationships. That and I hadn't met Charlotte until now.

It had taken me fifteen years to find someone like Charlotte, but now that I had met her, it all seemed worth the wait.

Even though I wanted to take my time and do things right with her, I also, at the same time, wanted to not waste any time.

That part of me wanted to rush ahead and get her to a justice of the peace.

Maybe I needed to have my head examined. My younger sister was a psychologist. I could call her. Get her to set me back on the right path.

My sister could remind me that I was a commitment avoider. Not a commitment phobic. Just a commitment avoider. Apparently there was a difference.

I would figure it out.

All I had to do was to go with my instinct.

This was uncharted territory.

I would take it one step at the time.

Chapter Twenty-Seven

CHARLOTTE

By eleven o'clock I had met four of my new students... or interns as they liked to be called.

They were excited and looking forward to begin painting the next day.

I instructed them to walk about the town today. To explore and just look around. Get an overall sense of the area. Then tomorrow we would focus.

I hadn't decided where we would start. I was thinking maybe that spot on the river where Bradford had taken me, but I wanted to work up to it. To start with something a bit easier. Maybe I'd start with one of the blue spruce trees off of main street. Get a sense of where the students were as far as their level of talent.

I sent William away, too. Told him to go exploring as well. I didn't tell him I had a lunch date.

As Noon approached, I started getting a little nervous. A little more nervous to be technical. I'd been nervous all morning.

Meeting the students had been a good distraction.

At a quarter to twelve, Bradford opened the door and stepped inside.

He stood there waiting for me to acknowledge him.

I stood up and going around my desk, walked toward him.

As I neared, he brought a long-stemmed rose from behind his back and held it out to me.

"Thank you," I said, pressing the soft rose petals against my cheek.

"A beautiful rose for a beautiful girl," he said. "Are you ready for lunch?"

"Yes. Just let me lock everything up." I logged out of my computer, grabbed my purse, and I was ready to go.

"Nice boots," he said as he held the door for me.

"My newest wardrobe staple," I said as I locked the door.

"I like a girl who can adapt," he said, taking my hand.

"Are we headed to the Hungry Biscuit?" I asked.

"If it's okay with you."

"I've already studied the menu so I'm ready to order."

He laughed. "I think I might be a bad influence on you."

We turned left and walked down the street. A woman watering an ivy outside her shop greeted us as we passed.

"Everyone seems so nice here," I said.

"Since we're both from the city, I guess it's a lot for us to get used to."

"I guess so. Have you ever thought about moving to a small town?"

"Why?" he asked. "Houston has everything I need. I have a high-rise apartment with a great view. There's always a good place to eat. Things to do."

"That's true," I said. "I don't take advantage of things like I guess I should."

"It's okay if you prefer to stay inside. You're like my older sister in that way."

We walked past a woman pushing a baby carriage. Bradford held the door for her while she pushed the carriage into the General Store.

She thanked him profusely.

"What's your sister like?" I asked. I was curious about what kind of family he was from. Unfortunately, his name had not been on the Skye Travels website at all.

"She's a full time mom and loves it."

"She's married then?"

"Yes. Married at eighteen. Married the guy she started dating when they were freshmen in high school.

"Wow. That's pretty amazing. What about you? No high school sweetheart for you?"

"No," he said. "I didn't date much until college. Turns out girls like a man in uniform."

"It's an interesting phenomenon, isn't it?"

"Hard to complain. How about you? Why aren't you hitched?"

I shrugged. "I just never wanted to put the time into it. I spent all my time either painting or reading."

"So you just kind of disappeared into the folds of your large family?"

I looked over at him. "You are quite perceptive," I said. "And yes."

He took my hand as we crossed the street and didn't let go.

We walked the last block to the Hungry Biscuit in silence.

"Have you been here before?"

"No. I haven't spent much time in Whiskey Springs until now."

"Huh. You seem to know a lot about it."

"I've been here. Overnight a couple of times. Just stayed at the saloon."

The hostess seated us at a table next to a window.

Soft music played in the background—quite a change from the piano music of the saloon which had actually grown on me.

We both set our menus aside without opening them.

"So," he said. "What are you thinking to order?"

"I'm thinking the burger and fries. Seems to be their specialty."

"Then that's what I'll have, too."

I was feeling comfortable with Bradford. He was not only a handsome pilot who was a good kisser, but he was a good companion.

Zoe suggested I not worry about crushing on him. Said it was normal.

Zoe would know. Zoe always had a boyfriend of some sort.

Me? I have to be careful about getting too involved. Since I didn't date, I had a tendency to fall faster.

Or so it seemed.

Maybe it was just Bradford.

Chapter Twenty-Eight

Bradford

The hamburgers and fries at the Hungry Biscuit lived up their reputation. Instead of ketchup, they served something they called fry sauce.

"I think it's an out west thing," I said when Charlotte asked me about it.

"I like it," she said. "It's like a mix of mayo and ketchup and something else I can't quite figure out."

"A secret ingredient," I said.

I knew so many people who weren't open to trying new things. I really liked it that Charlotte was.

As a pilot, I found myself in a lot of different places and different situations that required me to adapt. As such, I considered myself to be well rounded along with being adaptable. It was a useful quality.

"What do you do when you aren't flying?" Charlotte asked.

"Is there something other than flying?" I asked.

She laughed. "You really are like my brothers."

"It's a pilot thing."

"So it seems. But really. There has to be something else you like to do."

"I like movies. I know it sounds boring, but that's what I enjoy. For fun."

"It doesn't sound boring to me. I like movies, too, and I also like reading. People often think reading is really boring."

"Why would someone think that?" he asked.

"I don't know." Finished eating, I shoved my plate aside. "I guess because it isn't rock climbing or water skiing."

"Overrated," I said.

"You've done those things?"

"I guess I've tried just about everything once." I shoved my plate aside. "But." I held up a finger.

"But?"

"There is one thing I haven't done and I don't plan to do."

"What's that?" I leaned forward, curious about what a guy who had done just about everything wouldn't do.

"I refuse to jump out of a perfectly good airplane."

She looked at me a moment. Then she laughed.

"Coming from a pilot, that makes perfect sense."

"I'm glad you agree," I said.

"Wholeheartedly."

"Now if there was a problem with the airplane, I would jump out of it."

She nodded seriously. "I would certainly hope so."

The server came to our table. Gathered up our plates.

"Can I interest you in some fresh apple pie?" he asked.

"Do you like apple pie?" I asked.

"I love apple pie," I said. "Our cook makes the best."

"We'll have two apple pies ala mode," I told the server.

I sat back and studied Charlotte as she checked her phone messages.

She had just inadvertently revealed something very important about herself and I don't think she even realized it.

The girl not only came from a large family, but they had a cook. In fact, it sounded like they still had a cook.

I had some investigating to do.

I wanted to learn more about this girl who was running away with my heart.

Chapter Twenty-Nine

CHARLOTTE

While we waited for the server to bring our pie, I busied myself on my phone.

I knew that most people considered it rude to use their phone at the table, but I needed to give Bradford time to forget about what I had just told him.

I had just told him that we had a cook.

It wasn't a big deal. A lot people in Pittsburgh knew that the Ashtons had a cook.

I just hadn't told Bradford yet that my uncle owned the airline he worked for.

No matter how much I told myself it didn't matter, I didn't want it to confuse anything he and I had going.

I didn't want him to look at me differently.

I hoped he hadn't noticed it. He hadn't commented, so I took that as a good sign.

Later. I would tell him later. But right now, I was enjoying things being the way they were.

When the server brought our pie, I put my phone away.

"Everything okay?" he asked.

"Just one of the students asking what time he needed to show up in the morning."

"You're looking forward to your classes."

"Turns out it's more like an internship. We'll do some classwork, but mostly we'll be outside in the field painting."

"And you had nothing to do with organizing it?"

"No," I said, taking a bite of pie. "It would have been nice to have been part of it."

"So the students were chosen from applications... by someone."

I nodded.

"Did you apply?"

"No. I didn't. It's possible someone applied for me, but I don't know."

"Then you were chosen also."

"So it seems. Do you like your pie?" I nodded toward his plate. He'd barely touched it.

"It's good," he said, picking up his fork and taking his second bite. "I'm just trying to figure out how you ended up here."

"When you figure that out," I said. "Let me know."

"It's the Whiskey Springs magic," he said.

"Right." I laughed. "The Whiskey Springs magic."

Even though I laughed, a little shiver ran down my spine.

What if there was something to it? What if there was some kind of magic to Whiskey Springs?

It was overwhelming to think about how Bradford and I had ended up here in the same place at the same time.

Out of all the people in all the world in all the places, we ended up here. Together.

I picked up the red rose I'd laid on the table and inhaled deeply.

He was perfect for me... at this moment.

But I couldn't shake the feeling that I was just convenient for him.

We both knew we lived in different cities in different parts of the country, but when I looked into his blue eyes, I couldn't think about that.

When I looked into his eyes, the distance between us didn't seem to matter. It didn't seem to matter that we came from two different worlds.

I didn't want the evening to end.

I had no way of knowing when he would leave Whiskey Springs. He could be called away at any time.

"Penny for your thoughts," he said.

I looked away and shook my head.

"I was just thinking."

"Don't think too hard," he said, pressing a hand against mine.

"That's asking a lot."

"I know. It is for me, too."

Nodding, I looked away again.

"Do you want to go for a walk in the moonlight?" he asked. "A romantic stroll?"

"That sounds nice."

"Don't think so much," he said. "Everything is going to be okay."

I didn't know what he meant by that, but I found it odd that he seemed to sense that I was troubled.

Perhaps he was struggling, also with what we were going to do after this interlude passed.

That's what this was. It was a romantic interlude.

Sort of like a summer romance, except that it wasn't summer.

Lifting my chin, I smiled at him.

"I know," I said.

No matter what happened, it would be okay.

Chapter Thirty

BRADFORD

The wind was cool, but not as cold as it had been last night.

The weather was a bit unpredictable this time of year.

Charlotte and I walked hand-in-hand down Main Street back toward the saloon.

We walked slowly, neither one of us in any hurry to get back to the saloon.

Main Street was pretty much deserted with all the stores closed. The sidewalks were lined with old-fashioned street lights and blue spruce trees.

"What are you going to do all day tomorrow?" Charlotte asked. "While I'm working."

"Oh," I said, swinging her hand with mine. "I don't know. I'm afraid I'll be horribly bored."

"Are you on call? In case someone needs to fly somewhere?"

"Probably. But I don't expect that to happen. I'm here until further notice."

"Why?" she asked.

"I don't really know why."

"It's unusual, though, right?"

"A little." A lot.

I didn't want to think about it too much. If I thought about it too much, something might change.

We could hear the piano music before we reached the saloon.

"How long do they play?" she asked.

"I really don't know."

We stopped outside the door and looked out toward the mountains at the moonlight streaming over the peaks.

"This is quite a different view from what I'm used to," I said.

"What kind of view are you used to?"

"From my apartment I watch the sunrise over the city of Houston. I don't really see the sunset except for its reflection off of other glass buildings."

"Huh."

"What kind of view do you have?"

"We live just outside of Pittsburgh. We don't really have any neighbors."

"You live in the country?"

"No. Not the country."

The clouds shifted, drifting over the moon, obscuring our view of the mountains.

"It's a short drive."

"You live with your parents."

"My whole family lives together."

I didn't say anything as I tried to process that. Since she had a big family, I wasn't sure what she meant by her whole family. Surely she didn't mean that her five brothers and sisters and her parents lived in the same house.

"It's a big house," she said with a little sigh.

"And you have a cook."

"Yes. We have a cook."

I nodded slowly. "Just how big are we talking?"

"You know," she said. "The usual. Two wings. Eight bedrooms."

"So basically you live in a hotel."

She laughed. "Not that big."

The piano music stopped abruptly.

We looked at each other.

"That's different," I said, glancing at my phone. "It's not that late."

"They played until Midnight last night," she said. "I was awake."

"We should go inside. Check it out."

I couldn't keep her outside all night because as much as I wanted it to, time wasn't showing any signs of standing still.

Chapter Thirty-One

CHARLOTTE

The saloon had a different feel without the music. It seemed everyone talked in hushed tones.

A couple of people left as Bradford and I went inside. Maybe it was a coincidence or maybe they had come for the music.

Instead of going upstairs, we sat at a table not too far from the piano.

"What do you think happened?" I asked.

"Maybe something happened and she had to leave. Or the other person didn't show up."

"I can only imagine that it would be a scheduling nightmare."

A server came and dropped off a pitcher of water and two glasses. Asked if we wanted anything to drink.

"Sorry it's so quiet," the server said. "One of the girls called in sick."

"That must happen a lot," Bradford said.

"Not really," the server, a young man said. "Hasn't happened since I started working here six months ago."

"I hate that," Bradford said after the server walked away. "The music is what makes the saloon."

"It does seem like it, doesn't it? Do you play?"

"Me? No way. Music was never encouraged in our family."

"That's too bad," I said.

"What about your family?"

"We were actually encouraged to do anything we wanted."

He nodded slowly. "Like painting."

"Yes. Like painting." I looked up at him from beneath my lashes. "Excuse me for a minute."

I walked over the piano and sat down.

Waited a minute to see if anyone protested, but no one seemed to notice or care.

Bradford had followed me and stood leaning against the piano like a protector.

I looked at him questioningly.

He nodded.

I placed my fingers on the keys and started playing.

Once I started, I forgot to be worried about what anyone thought.

I lost myself in the music and didn't look up until I'd played a whole song.

When I stopped, everyone in the saloon started clapping.

Putting my hands in my lap, I bowed my head.

"Don't stop," Bradford said. "You have fans now."

"My music is a little bit different from what they're used to here."

"And you think that matters," he said, moving to sit next to me.

"You said you don't play."

"Doesn't mean I can't watch, does it?"

"No," I said slowly. "But... you might make me nervous."

"I never want to make you nervous," he said, sweeping a lock of hair away from my face.

"Right," I said. Surely he knew that wasn't helping. He had to know that it didn't help.

Taking a deep breath, I laid my fingers back on the keys.

Why not?

It had been awhile since I'd played the piano and even longer since I'd played for an audience.

I mentally ran through the songs I knew by heart and chose my favorite, a hauntingly sad song.

I closed my eyes as my fingers flew over the keys. Everything else faded into the background. Even Bradford. Almost.

When I finished the song, the music still hanging in the air, I turned and looked into his smiling blue eyes.

"You are absolutely stunningly amazing," he said.

I shrugged. "It's nothing."

"Nothing? Right."

Leaning forward, he kissed me.

Chapter Thirty-Two

BRADFORD

With the strains of the piano music still lingering in the air, I leaned forward and kissed Charlotte.

She was truly the most stunning woman I had ever met.

She was not only an artist, no doubt talented. I hadn't seen her work, but she was a professor so she had to be talented. She could play the piano like a angel.

And she had the beauty of an elfin princess including the guileless smile that went with it. When she smiled, her whole face lit up like sunshine.

I was about as smitten as a man could be.

My phone chimed in my pocket, but I ignored it.

Right now all I cared about was Charlotte.

But I had to move carefully. Respectfully.

"You have a busy day tomorrow," I said. "I should get you to your room."

"Right," she said, clearing her throat and looking away. "Of course."

Was that disappointment on her face? I did not want to disappoint her, but at the same time, I was afraid that if I didn't walk her to her room now, I'd never want to let her out of my sight.

As we walked across the room toward the stairs leading up to the rooms, I recognized the manager, a man named Franklin Moore, approaching us.

"Excuse me," he said, looking from one of us to the other. He looked rather disconcerted.

"It's okay Franklin," I said. "What's wrong?"

"So sorry to bother you," he said. "But Noah Worthington is on the phone."

That explained who had been calling me.

"Wait here a moment," I said to Charlotte. "I just need to take this call."

"No," Franklin said. "He is asking for Charlotte."

"Charlotte? Why?" I looked at Charlotte, but she looked as confused as I felt.

"I'll be right back," she said.

I watched her walk toward the office behind the bar with Franklin to answer the phone.

To answer a call from Noah Worthington.

Why would Noah be calling Charlotte?

Perplexed, I sat down on the nearest barstool to wait.

"Can I get you something, Sir?" the bartender asked.

"A glass of water," I said absently.

When he slid a glass of water my way, I drank it automatically without thinking.

To say that I was confused would be an understatement.

I pulled out my phone and checked my missed calls.

It had not been Noah calling. It had been my older sister. She'd left a message just checking in. She did that quite often. I should really call her more often. She was a good sister, trying to hold our family together.

A couple of minutes later, Charlotte came back out of the office.

"Everything okay?" I asked.

"Everything is great," she said, taking my hand as we started up the stairs.

"Noah Worthington called you," I said as we neared the top of the stairs.

"Yeah…" she said. "I think he's the one who set up this internship."

"Why do you think that?"

We reached her door and stopped.

"He wanted to know how it was going."

I leaned against the wall next to her door, looking at her for some answer to this mystery, but she didn't seem the least bit concerned.

"I think I'm missing a piece of this puzzle."

"Probably," she said, looking toward the ceiling as though she would find answers there.

"And?"

As she looked into my eyes, I saw the hesitation there.

"I guess it's okay to tell you," she said. "He's my Uncle Noah."

Chapter Thirty-Three

BRADFORD

Moonlight spilled in through my window. I liked the curtains open. Something to do with living in a high rise, no doubt. There was no need to close the curtains in a high rise and I had gotten used to having not the moonlight, but also the city lights spilling through my window at night, not to mention the abundance of natural light during the day.

After untying my shoes and tugging them off, I paced the bedroom in my socks.

Everything had fallen into place in one fell swoop.

I couldn't quite figure out how I had missed it.

Her last name was Ashton. Noah Worthington and Charlotte's grandfather were brothers.

I vaguely remembered when that all went down, but I honestly hadn't paid all that much attention to it. I hadn't figured it was my business at the time.

Had I known about Charlotte, I might would have paid more attention to the details.

Noah Worthington and Cole Ashton were brothers.

Something had gone down when they were young men that led Cole to change his name and vanish off the face of the earth.

For years... and years... Noah had not known whether his brother was even alive.

Then something happened. I'm not sure. I think that Cole Ashton had a heart attack and they reconnected.

So Charlotte was related to Noah. That meant Charlotte was basically an heiress.

Noah had plenty of children and grandchildren, but Charlotte's family was wealthy also.

Apparently successful entrepreneurship ran in the family.

Charlotte seemed to think that Noah had orchestrated this whole internship thing.

It made sense, knowing Noah's affinity for Whiskey Springs.

What I didn't understand was why.

Why would he set this whole thing up? Was it for Charlotte?

It wasn't for me and Charlotte. I wasn't supposed to be her pilot.

I stopped and looked out at the mountaintops in the moonlight.

Maybe it hadn't been chance after all.

They said his grandson who was originally supposed to be Charlotte's pilot got a stomach virus at the last minute.

Not being a paranoid man, I hadn't thought much of that at the time. But now, looking back, maybe there was no stomach virus after all.

Maybe I was supposed to be the pilot all along.

I'd heard rumors that Noah Worthington had a tendency to play Cupid.

Had he played Cupid with me and Charlotte?

That was one of the most far-fetched things I could imagine.

It was even more far-fetched, or at least as far-fetched as my belief in the magic of Whiskey Springs.

It was different though.

The magic of a small town was different from thinking that Noah Worthington had gone to this much trouble to bring me and Charlotte together.

He wouldn't even have any way of knowing if we would like each other.

The whole idea was fanciful.

It was just a coincidence.

I untied my tie and slid it out from around my neck, then hung it up in the bureau that served as a closet.

At the end of the day, it didn't really matter how Charlotte and I ended up here together.

The only thing that mattered was that we did.

And since we were here together, then all I had to do was to make the most of it.

I would court Charlotte to the best of my ability and then after our time together here was up, I would figure out how to keep her in my life.

Fortunately I didn't have to know right now how that might

happen, but I had faith that I would somehow figure something out when it was time.

Chapter Thirty-Four

CHARLOTTE

I had a good group of students. Twelve of them from all over the country.

I found it baffling that Noah had all this set up without me knowing about it.

He knew I was an artist and he knew I was a professor.

It was possible that he had chosen me to be here all along. In fact, the more I thought about it, the more I believed that had to be what happened.

After spending an hour or so getting to know the students and going over some of the things we would be doing over the next couple of months, William distributed canvases and easels and paints and brushes and smocks and we all headed outside.

It was a beautiful fall day. The sun was warm on our heads, but the wind kept it from feeling warm at all. Probably a good way to end up with a sunburn.

I'd chosen a spot in a little park just off Main Street with lots of colorful aspen and maple trees as the first project for my students to paint.

I instructed them not to try to paint an ambitious landscape to start out. Not a panoramic scene that included trees and mountain tops in the background. To just pick one thing, maybe a tree, to start.

I had a feeling most of them would be more ambitious and try to paint more. If they did, that would be okay. I wanted to get a sense of where they were with their abilities.

Tomorrow I might bring a canvas for myself and do some painting, but not today. Today I wandered around and watched them.

They were all quite talented and it looked like they were only going to need a few pointers here and there.

As I wandered around the park, weaving among the dozen or so artists, I noticed that I watched the road.

I watched for Bradford.

He'd been understandably confused about why Noah would call me. He hadn't been alone in that. I had been confused too, but it hadn't taken me long to figure it out.

Bradford, on the other hand, seemed especially disconcerted. Part of it might have been because I hadn't told him that Noah was my uncle.

I probably should have.

I was going to.

I was just waiting for the right time. I didn't want anything with him to change. Everything had been going so well.

Sometimes when people found out who I was, they acted differently.

Fortunately, very few people put it together that my grandfather was Cole Ashton, real estate mogul.

Grandpa Cole tended to stay out of the limelight. That helped.

And no one in the university expected Cole Ashton's granddaughter to work there as a professor or even as an administrator.

As such, that had never been a problem for me.

As it neared lunchtime, I sent William into town for sandwiches for everyone and we ate at the little picnic tables there in the park.

As we ate, I couldn't stop watching for Bradford. Oddly enough, we'd hardly been apart since we'd left Pittsburgh.

I had no doubt that he could find me if he wanted to. My large group of students wouldn't be hard to track.

Maybe he'd been called out on a flight.

Or maybe he had found something else to do.

Either way, I didn't see him all day.

I couldn't say that I was happy about that.

Not happy at all.

But, of course, I had a job to do.

I shouldn't be worrying about my handsome pilot.

Even if he had swept me off my feet.

Chapter Thirty-Five

BRADFORD

I started off my day the way I always did. With a cup of coffee in my hands while I watched the sunrise.

I resolved to leave Charlotte alone today. Her classes—or internship—as she called it were starting up. She needed to focus.

Fourteen people wandering the town would have been hard to miss even if I hadn't been looking for them.

I was in the General Store shopping for toothpaste when they walked past, all carrying easels and canvases and bags that no doubt held paints, brushes, and smocks.

They were a quiet group, still getting to know each other.

Charlotte and William were in the lead.

They had lunch—sandwiches—in the park, then went back to work. I admired their focus, but I could relate to it.

They were artists, just as I was a pilot.

And like me, they were passionate about what they did.

I was surprised that Maggie at Skye Travels hadn't sent me on a flight yet.

For some very odd reason, I was being left alone. Typically someone would need the airplane and me to fly it. Maybe it was a slow week.

And it wasn't like Charlotte was going to need a ride back to Pittsburgh anytime soon.

My nonsuspicious nature was a bit suspicious about the whole thing.

I didn't mind, though.

I used the time to think about Charlotte and to plan activities for us.

It was harder to come up with things in Whiskey Springs. If we were in Houston, it would be easy. In Houston I could take her to a play or the orchestra or to see the butterflies.

Here I had to pretty much rely on nature instead.

It took a bit more work for me. We could take a hike along the river. Have a picnic.

There was a place just outside of town where we could go horseback riding. I'd never been on a horse, but that was okay. Charlotte probably hadn't been on a horse either. We would learn together.

There was a movie theatre in town, but they only had a couple of movies playing at any given time.

Since I'd already flown into Boulder for dinner, I had to pace myself on that one. Be more creative.

As the afternoon dragged past, I kept an eye on the time. I

considered going to her office and waiting, but instead, I wandered back toward the saloon.

Going to her office seemed a little too presumptuous.

I found a table next to the window in the saloon and ordered myself a coke.

Things in the saloon were back to normal. There was a girl wearing a long ruffled 1800s-era dress playing the piano, her hair pulled high on her head with a little feather woven into it.

It just made me miss Charlotte all the more.

Charlotte's music was better. From what I'd heard, Charlotte could have played professionally, but she had chosen to be a university professor and an artist.

After what seemed like forever, but was actually only a few minutes later, the group of art students came wandering back along the other side of the street. They were already pairing up. Making friends.

I didn't see Charlotte. Not at first anyway.

She was coming along behind the students, walking with a tall lanky man with blonde hair sweeping his shoulders.

The man talked animatedly using his hands and Charlotte was nodding. They were obviously in a deep conversation. Probably about art.

The man looked like a quintessential artist. Something clenched in my stomach.

I hadn't considered that Charlotte would make other artist friends. Of course she would. I shouldn't be surprised.

She would have things in common with another artist. They would have things to talk about that I wouldn't even have a clue about.

Charlotte didn't even so much as look up as she walked past. She was listening intently to what Artist Guy was saying.

Feeling like I had missed something, I sat back in my chair and tapped my glass. I no longer wanted the coke. I'd lost my taste for it.

The server came, but I waved her away. Taking a couple of dollars from my wallet, I left them on the table and went upstairs to my room where I proceeded to pace again.

Maybe I should just leave Charlotte alone.

I had just assumed that she would want to hang out with me. Maybe Artist Guy was someone she already knew. Maybe they were friends.

Having twisted myself up into a knot, I could hardly think straight.

Finally, I sent Maggie at Skye Travels a message.

> How long do you think I'll be waiting here?

Maggie wrote right back.

> MAGGIE
> Not sure. Why?

> Just curious. Not much to do here.

And the girl I had fallen for had gone back into the fold of other artists. She had already made a new friend, perhaps even a new boyfriend. Someone who spoke her language.

MAGGIE

Let me check. I'll get back to you. It was my understanding you were there for two months.

I didn't think you were serious about that.

MAGGIE

Hold tight. I'll find out.

I slid my phone back into my pocket and left my room. I needed to take a walk.

Chapter Thirty-Six

CHARLOTTE

One of the students was a couple of years older than me. An untraditional student named Harold.

I often attracted what I thought of as groupies. Students who liked to hang around with me outside of class. Often telling me about their personal ambitions. Or their history. Or, in Harold's case, both.

He had held me up showing me pictures of some of the paintings he had done in the past. They were a little too dark for my taste, but I didn't want to be rude. So I looked at them with him.

Finally, I told him that I had to meet the other students at the office.

We walked past the saloon to the office on Main Street where the other students were already putting their supplies away.

William, bless his heart, was there doing an awesome job of coordinating everything.

"William," I said. "I'm glad you're still here. I need to go over a couple of things before you leave."

"Sure. Dr. Ashton."

He waited while Harold put away his supplies.

"See you tomorrow, Harold," I said, hoping he would understand that he was supposed to leave now.

He hesitated, but glanced at me, then William.

"Alright," he said. "Have a good night, Doc."

After the door closed behind Harold, I blew out a breath of relief.

"I'm heading back to the saloon. Walk with me?"

"Sure. What did you want to talk to me about?"

After I locked up the office, William and I started down the street toward the saloon.

"I just wanted to thank you for all your help today," I said.

"Just doing my job," William said.

I couldn't say that was my favorite phrase, but that was just on me. To me work was more than just doing a job.

"How do you think things went today?" I asked him.

"I think things went okay. Makes me wish I'd majored in art." William was a psychology major who had taken an art appreciation class with me. Creative endeavors weren't his strengths, but he was organized and he was loyal. Two things that made me appreciate having him as a graduate student.

I laughed. "I can imagine. Made me want to paint something, too."

We reached the saloon and stepped inside. I knew that fortunately the students weren't staying in the saloon. They were all staying in a motel just outside of town, though still within walking distance. One of the benefits of such a small town.

"I'll see you in the morning, William," I said.

William headed over to the bar while I headed upstairs. I wanted to get a shower after being outside all day and change clothes.

While the hot water ran over my head, I wondered where Bradford had been all day. What had he done?

I'd thought he would have at least stopped by to see what we were doing.

I had to remind myself that he wasn't a boyfriend. I couldn't expect him to just drop by for no reason.

But that was the whole problem. I wanted him to be my boyfriend.

He'd acted like a boyfriend since we'd left Pittsburgh, so why would he suddenly decide not to be.

I'd probably just missed seeing him.

I spent some time drying my hair with a round brush, smoothing it out.

We hadn't set plans for today, but that didn't mean that we couldn't have any.

Maybe we were already at the point where we didn't have to make plans ahead of time.

I rather liked that idea.

By the time I got my hair dried, it was just about time for dinner. Early, but not too early.

I paced to the window and looked out over the back lawn. The sun was starting to set over the mountains.

I realized that I had been looking forward all day to watching the sunset with Bradford.

I paced across the floor again to the door, then back to the window.

At the window, I turned and paced back to the door.

This was not going to do.

It was not going to do at all.

I opened the door and walked out into the hallway.

Turning right, I stopped at the door next to mine and before I could talk myself out of it, I knocked.

Then I held my breath.

I imagined Bradford walking across the room and opening the door.

But Bradford didn't come to the door.

While I waited I looked down at the customers in the saloon below. Sitting at the tables. On the barstools.

I scanned every face down there, looking for Bradford. Thinking… hoping perhaps… that I had missed him when I came through earlier.

But he wasn't down there. If he was, I would see him.

Committed now, I turned and knocked again.

He wasn't coming to the door.

This was not what I had planned.

Chapter Thirty-Seven

BRADFORD

By the time I got to the river, I realized I had overreacted.

Red and gold leaves floated past in the rushing river below, the roar of the water somehow clearing my thoughts.

Of course Charlotte's students would want to talk to her. She was their professor.

She was knowledgeable and friendly. Approachable.

Truth was she was pretty much the only thing I had thought about all day long.

I'd thought about what she and I could do together.

I'd spent time on the Internet. I'd walked around. I'd even talked to a couple of people who lived in town who might know what kind of things there were to do around here.

Someone suggested we go out and visit a maple syrup farm even though it wasn't maple sap season. That sounded interesting so I'd put it on my mental list of things for us to do.

A bighorn sheep wandered down to the river, took a drink of water, then stood, his head held high as he sniffed the air.

I'd go back to my hotel room. Take a shower.

Then I'd go next door and talk Charlotte into getting dinner with me. Maybe we'd even eat downstairs in the saloon.

Something easy. Unplanned.

All I really wanted to do was talk to her anyway.

The sun was starting to set, so I left my perch on the rock at the river's edge and started back.

I'd no more than reached the ground when my phone rang.

It was Maggie in Houston.

"Hey," she said. "Good news."

Uh oh. Suddenly good news wasn't going to be good news. I'd asked her to get me out of here. If she had, then she had bad news.

"We got a call from Mr. St. Clair of Whiskey Springs who just so happens to need a flight out."

"Ok," I said. It was a reminder that I had to be careful what I asked for. I walked beneath a grove of aspen trees, their golden leaves quaking in the wind.

"When?" It would be okay if it was while Charlotte was working. It would give me something to do to get my mind off of her.

"Tonight," Maggie said.

I stopped right there in the middle of the trail.

"Tonight?"

"Yes. It was quite fortuitous, actually that you just happen to be there. With an airplane."

"Yes. Fortuitous."

I started walking again. Slowly now.

"What time can you meet him at the airport?"

Maybe I misunderstood.

"I'll check the weather," I said, grasping for a delay. "Is the morning an option for him?"

"The radar checks out. You're good. Tonight. You can be back in Houston tonight."

This was the last time I was going to make any rash decisions, certainly any rash messages.

Ever.

"Let me check and I'll get back to you."

It was an odd statement to come out of my mouth. Like most pilots, my usual answer was "Just tell me what time to be there."

But this was not the usual anything.

I disconnected the phone and kept walking.

I didn't have anything to check, unless my emotions counted.

There was really no choice. I had no choice. Not now.

I should have left things alone.

Maggie would have found another solution if I hadn't called her asking for a way out of here.

This was not one of my best moments.

I needed to find Charlotte. Tell her I had to take a flight.

But I would be back.

I would find a way back.

Chapter Thirty-Eight

CHARLOTTE

Not wanting to stay in my room, I took my iPad and went down the street to the coffee shop. They had good Wi Fi and I had a slew of emails to answer.

It was a good distraction to keep me from thinking about Bradford.

He and I should have exchanged phone numbers. How had we not done that most basic of things? Not with as much time as we had spent together.

I soon lost myself in my emails. With classes starting back, I had emails from students and even though I was here, I still had assistant director duties—paperwork—that had to be done.

It hadn't taken me long to learn that assistant was synonymous with paperwork. They should just call the position Assistant Paperwork Person.

Being outside today, among the artists busy at work, had brought to my attention just how much of an artist I was. That and a professor.

I missed working with the students.

I was a professor and an artist. I'd only taken the promotion to assistant director of the college of arts and sciences because I'd wanted my family to be proud of me. They had all congratulated me afterwards and the whole family had gone out to dinner to celebrate.

In retrospect, I think they thought I wanted the promotion. Of course they would think it. I was the one who took it, right?

Finished up with the emails, I made some notes on my students. I already had their names memorized. It was something I always made a point to do. The students were always surprised I knew their names after the first day.

It wasn't that hard to do and with just twelve, it was a breeze.

I stopped working long enough to look up. My coffee cup was empty and the sun was already heading down. It was time for me to pack up and go back to the hotel.

Maybe Bradford was back by now. Maybe he'd been taking a nap. It was possible. My oldest brother was like that. He could sleep through anything.

Walking back along Main Street, the tall mountains in the distance, I definitely understood the allure. White wispy clouds floated along toward the mountains towering around us. Whiskey Springs was already high in elevation. Over nine thousand feet. And yet the mountains still towered above us. It was awe-inspiring.

And I wanted to capture it all on canvas.

I heard the piano music drifting from the saloon before I reached the door.

As I walked across toward the stairs, I recognized Franklin, the manager, behind the bar. He waved me over.

"I have a message for you," he said.

"Who from?" I instinctively checked my phone to make sure it was turned on. Anyone who would be trying to get in touch with me should have my cell phone number. Except, of course, Noah. I wasn't sure why he'd called me here at the saloon. He could easily get my cell phone number.

"Bradford," he said.

And Bradford. Bradford was the other exception.

"What's the message?" I asked.

"He wanted me to let you know that he had to take an unexpected flight out tonight. But he'll be back."

I just stared at him. An unexpected flight. That explained where he had gone.

"Thank you," I murmured. Then added over my shoulder as I walked away. "Did he say when?"

"No ma'am."

So Bradford wasn't here. He'd left to go on a flight.

I felt like a cloud had settled over my world, turning everything dreary and drab.

Chapter Thirty-Nine

BRADFORD

After arriving back in Houston, my schedule automatically filled up.

My days were consumed with flights for the next eight days.

I went to Atlanta. New Orleans. Dallas three times. Lafayette. And back to Atlanta. Then Austin.

It was like my time in Whiskey Springs had never happened. Except that I couldn't stop thinking about Charlotte.

I kicked myself daily for asking to leave Whiskey Springs.

Everything had been idyllic while I was there.

I'd no more than landed in Austin when I got a text from a girl I usually saw when I was in Austin. Not a girlfriend, really. My Austin girlfriend maybe.

DALIA
Hey there.

What was she doing? Tracking my phone? It was too coincidental for her to text me the moment I landed. Not during my flight either. Those messages had already come in.

I started not to answer, but that seemed wrong. She and I always had a good time together.

> Hi

DALIA
Will you be back in Austin soon?

I had the distinct feeling that she already knew the answer to that, but I couldn't figure out how. I didn't go around giving anyone permission to track my phone.

I didn't answer right away. Instead, I escorted my passenger out making sure he made it to the car that drove up for him, then went through my post flight checklist.

DALIA
Want to have dinner?

Dalia had just given herself away as far as I was concerned. She knew I was in Austin.

I went through my phone, looking for evidence that Dalia or anyone for that matter could be tracking my phone.

Typically landing in Austin automatically meant dinner with Dalia.

Since my client was a drop off, my routine was to have dinner with Dalia then I would fly back to Houston.

The truth was, I didn't have the stomach for having dinner with Dalia.

My heart was with Charlotte and having dinner with Dalia felt too much like cheating on Charlotte.

> I can't. Heading back to Houston.

I went into the terminal. Grabbed a sandwich and a coke. Then went back aboard my airplane and logged in my return flight to Houston.

I felt lighter already.

And this conversation, such that it was, with Dalia was enlightening.

As I checked the radar looking for weather problems, I admitted to myself that there was only one girl I was interested in having dinner with. Dinner or anything else.

And that girl was currently in Whiskey Springs.

And since she just so happened to be my boss's niece, there was no reason for me to suffer in silence.

I knew where to find her. All I had to do was make it happen.

"Cleared for takeoff."

The control tower's command was music to my ears.

It would be late when I got back to Houston so I went ahead and sent a message to Maggie.

> Would you set up a meeting for me with Noah in the morning?

As I took off down the runway, picking up speed and gaining ground effect, I got a response from Maggie just before I lost cell phone service.

MAGGIE

Done

Chapter Forty

CHARLOTTE

The next ten days passed slowly.

The air was a little cooler in the evenings and there were a couple of cloudy days that had us all wearing jackets.

I watched for Bradford at every turn.

All I knew was what Franklin had told me.

Bradford would be back.

That didn't mean he would be back today or this week. It just meant he would be back.

As the days passed, I came to the conclusion that he had not meant it literally. It was just what people said. Like "I'll see you around."

There was no definite time on it.

And certainly no guarantee.

So I threw myself into my work.

I actually painted a landscape that I was rather pleased with.

Since today was Saturday, I decided to head out on my own to do some painting. The students were off today, free to do whatever they pleased. I'd heard some of them talking about driving into Boulder. Others were planning a hike. Harold was driving home. Thank goodness. He took up far too much of my time and energy with his tales. He was a bit of a showoff too.

I went by the office and gathered up my supplies. An easel. A fresh canvas. Paints and brushes.

Wearing my new hiking boots that reminded me of Bradford, I stopped by the coffee shop for a coffee and a muffin for later in case I got hungry. Typically when I was painting, though, I didn't eat.

The breeze had a definite chill to it, but I didn't mind. The brisk temperatures were invigorating.

I went to the boulder at the edge of the river where Bradford had taken me on our first walk.

I gave some thought to climbing up, but I didn't think it would be a good place set up my easel. So I found a flat place next to the river and set up.

I'd brought a small easel, so I spread a blanket on the ground and made myself comfortable.

I never got tired of making that first streak of paint on a blank canvas. A blank canvas held so many possibilities.

I could capture anything in front of me on the canvas.

I started with the mountains in the background. Captured the white clouds clustering around them. The sky blue in the background.

This time out here in Whiskey Springs was enlightening.

I'd started out with a new friend. Bradford. I'd started falling for him the moment I first saw him.

I thought about him all the time. Replaying his kisses about a million times.

I didn't need a history of dating a lot of different men to know that he was different. To know that he was the one for me.

He had awakened emotions in me that I didn't even know I had.

Then there were the students. I'd enjoyed being back hands on with them. Helping them. Guiding them.

And on top of all that, there was my art. Reconnecting with my art was no small thing. No small thing at all.

As I dabbed my brush into a bit of light blue paint, I felt a reconnection with my love of painting.

Granted. I had a lot of talents. I could play the piano. I could beat any one of my brothers in a game of pool. But splashing paint on a canvas was my jam.

It was what I'd been born to do.

Maybe I had gotten off track as the years went by. I'd taken a job teaching at the university because it was expected that I have a career—a paying career—and it was the one career that allowed me to continue my art.

I had harbored the misperception that being a college professor would give me more time to paint.

That had been a myth. From the outside, being a professor looked completely different than it did from the inside.

On the inside, there was actually very little time left over after the responsibilities were completed to spend painting. And when there was time, there was no energy to go with it.

Being a college professor was exhausting work, especially for an introvert like me.

I needed time alone like I was having right now to energize. That was the classic definition of being an introvert. It had nothing to do with being socially awkward which I was not.

Maybe it was time I made some changes in my life.

Maybe I would resign from being assistant director of the college of arts and sciences.

It wasn't really my thing. They obviously didn't need me there. If they did, they wouldn't have agreed to send me here for eight weeks.

In all fairness, I didn't think they had a choice. Uncle Noah had set this up. I couldn't begin to fathom his motivation, but whatever it was, I was certain he had a reason.

Maybe it didn't really matter.

What mattered was that coming here had allowed me to indulge in a rare moment of introspection. What I found was that I needed this reconnection to my art.

What I did about that next I wasn't sure about yet. Not prone to rash decisions, I would take time to think about that.

I had no reason to do anything hasty.

I stopped moving and watched when three elk stepped out of the trees on the other side of the river and leisurely made their way across the meadow.

This was the kind of place where a person could go to heal.

I would give it some time.

My broken heart would heal.

It might have been broken here, but it could heal here as well.

Chapter Forty-One

BRADFORD

I couldn't say how I knew where to find her. Not really. It was a gut feeling.

In the ten days I had been gone, the weather had turned colder. Most of the colorful leaves were on the ground. Leaf peeping season was over.

The fall festival would be next. I'd seen a flyer for it at the saloon when I'd checked in.

Next would be the holidays. People would come here from all over the country for the lights and other festivities that came with the holidays.

That was something I wanted to do with Charlotte.

But I was getting ahead of myself again.

When I decided on doing something, I didn't wait.

Sometimes, like when I had asked Maggie to get me out of Whiskey Springs, it might have been a bit—a lot—contraindicated. Usually, however, it worked out well for me.

I didn't believe in letting opportunities pass me by.

Charlotte sat next to the rushing river where I had brought her that first time we had gone walking.

Instead of sitting on the boulder that would put her out over the water, she sat on the ground. She sat on a blanket, a small easel in front of her, a canvas propped on it.

She was wearing a smock and her hair was pulled back messily on top of her head, several strands falling unnoticed around her face.

Sitting very still, holding a brush in one hand, she watched three elk across the river.

I smiled.

This was exactly the kind of view I had hoped to share with her.

I liked it that she was alone. No Artist Guy with her. No students at all.

I'd thought of several things I could say to her, but I couldn't say that I had any kind of specific plan.

Sometimes a man had to fly by the seat of his pants.

I was quiet, so she must have sensed me standing behind her.

She looked over her shoulder at me and blinked.

A range of emotions raced over her face. Surprise. Disbelief. Then a smile.

The smile struck me straight in the heart.

She didn't move as I closed the distance between us.

"Hi," I said, standing in front of her.

"Hi." She said it so softly, I barely heard her against the roar of the river.

I knelt in front of her.

"Do you mind some company?" I asked.

"What took you so long?"

I shook my head.

"That's a good question."

I placed my fingers lightly beneath her chin and leaned forward to press my lips against hers.

"Is it okay with you if I stay?" I asked, my breath mingling with hers.

She obviously knew that I meant more than staying for this particular moment.

"What about your job?"

"I have connections."

She smiled. "Uncle Noah."

"Did you know that he orchestrated this whole thing?"

Her eyes widened.

"How is that possible?" she asked.

"I think he has some kind of superpower."

"Okay," she said.

"Okay?"

"Okay. You can stay."

I pulled her into my arms, not caring that we were getting light blue paint all over my white shirt.

I didn't care one bit.

Not even a little.

I was here. With Charlotte. And I wasn't going anywhere.

Epilogue

CHARLOTTE
December

The first week of December was crowded for Whiskey Springs and it would just get even more crowded as Christmas neared. The Christmas decorating competition. They would bring out the little narrow gauge train. Every inch of the town would light up with twinkling lights.

Snow fell lightly as we walked along Main Street toward the edge of town where they held the Fall Festival.

"Did you know that this is the first year they left the Ferris wheel up for Christmas?" I asked.

"I did not know that." Bradford said, squeezing my hand. "Is it a good one?"

"Is it a good what?"

"A good Ferris wheel?"

"I don't know. I've never ridden one."

He stopped and looked at me.

"Wait. You've never ridden on a Ferris wheel?"

"No," I said with a little laugh.

"Well," he said. "We have to fix that."

He took off toward the Ferris wheel, pulling me along with him.

Fifteen minutes later, with light snow falling, he had me sitting in one of the Ferris wheel cars.

"Are you sure this is safe?" I asked. It didn't feel particularly safe. It shifted and swayed with every movement, however small.

"You're asking a man who flies airplanes for a living?"

"Yes," I said, blinking innocently. "You seem like one who would be qualified to answer."

He laughed and pulled me close.

"Yes," he said. "I think it's safe enough."

"Safe enough," I said, wondering if it was too late to get out.

But we were already moving.

We moved slowly, going higher and higher.

I squeezed Bradford's hand.

When we reached the top, we stopped.

"What's wrong?" I asked. "Is it stuck?"

Bradford laughed.

"I asked the tech to stop it up here so we could have some time to look around."

"Oh," I said, relaxing and doing just that. I blinked as a snowflake landed on one of my eyelashes.

"It's beautiful," I said, looking out toward the winding river. It was a little like flying except different.

It was different from flying because we weren't moving.

With the snow falling and the mountains in the background on one side, the little town just visible over the trees, it looked like a painting.

"Whiskey Springs might be a nice place to live," I said.

"We can live wherever you want to live."

I turned and looked at him.

"We?" I repeated, my throat dry.

Somehow, in this small Ferris wheel car, he got on his knees.

"There's something I've been wanting to ask you," he said.

I was having trouble catching my breath.

His blue eyes were locked on mine. Blue eyes that rivaled the bluest of skies.

"Will you marry me?" He blurted it out like he had been holding it in and couldn't say it soon enough.

I couldn't stop the tears that sprang to my eyes and spilled over. I didn't even try.

They were happy tears.

I nodded. I nodded, but I couldn't speak.

"Yes?" he asked, grinning at me.

"Yes." I managed to get out.

Then I was in his arms and the Ferris wheel was moving again.

The Ferris wheel might be moving, but I was still on top of the world.

With Bradford, anything was possible.

Anything and everything was possible.

I had found my forever.

Keep Reading for a preview of Accidentally Forever...

AUTHOR OF PERFECTLY MISMATCHED

KATHRYN KALEIGH

Accidentally Forever

THE ASHTONS
FOREVER AND EVER

Preview

Chapter 1

Grace Miller

Just one more patient and I could call it a day.

I sat at my desk with my back to the window. On purpose. Too many distractions to try to work facing the window. I usually even lowered the shades when patients were in my office.

This fifth floor office had a clear view of the 610 West Loop looking out toward River Oaks. I couldn't see downtown Houston from here, but if I went up on the roof I could. From here downtown was so far away, it looked like a tiny cluster of buildings. Something a child might have built out of blocks.

No one went on the roof this time of year. Full on August in Houston was not the time for taking a break on the roof even if it had nice seating to enjoy the nice view. The building managers were talking about making the rooftop a green space with orange trees, but so far no one had moved in that direction.

Slipping my heels off, I rested my bare feet on the tops of my shoes. I wore what I considered appropriately conservative work attire. A dark gray pencil skirt with a matching blazer that hit at my waist. A white collared shirt. And of course, my heels.

I dragged the comb out of my hair and let my long hair swirl around my shoulders as I stretched my arms and got the blood flowing.

I had one hour to sit at my desk and catch up on notes for the day. I opened up my laptop and logged into the charting program my business partner insisted we use.

Me? I was okay with notes typed into a Word document and printed out supplemented by my handwritten notes neatly filed in folders and kept in a locked filing cabinet. A system that had served me well for the two years I'd had my own practice.

But going in with Jonathan had been a smart business move. He had more experience which meant he had more patients and not just that. He was on staff with the mental hospital and got frequent referrals. More than he could handle.

That's where I came in. I'd been with Jonathan for three months now and I was steadily building my patient load. At the rate I was going, Jonathan was going to have to bring in another psychologist before long.

He would have to lease another office if he did that and probably hire a receptionist. I had his old office and he had taken an empty larger one down the hall. There wasn't really space for a receptionist, but he would figure it out.

I was already working late at least three nights a week, one of them being tonight. I had to decide if I wanted to add Saturdays or another late night.

The office space was in a recently renovated building with freshly painted walls and hardwood floors. Very clean. Very modern.

I tried to make sure my space wasn't intimidating. I kept a cinnamon and vanilla candle lit and fresh flowers, currently white daisies, on the corner of my desk. I personally preferred the scent of daffodils, but the florist had been out when I'd stopped by this morning. Daisies were fine though.

This side of the office was what I considered the working side. Desk and a small bookcase with books I used often including the DSM.

The other side of the office was the therapeutic side. Two comfortable chairs and a love seat. One of the chairs was mine. I let the patients choose whether they wanted to sit on the sofa or the other chair.

No coffee table between us. Just a big bookcase with books that were more likely to appeal to patients. Self-help books, mostly. A strong believer in bibliotherapy, I kept it well stocked with my favorite books that I tended to give away.

All part of the cost of doing business.

I was fairly fast at charting, so I was well into my last patient's notes when my phone alarm went off, reminding me to get ready for my seven o'clock patient.

All I knew about him was that he was a twenty-seven-year-old male. I usually had a diagnosis when they were referrals from the hospital, but this man had self-referred through our website.

I saved everything on the computer, logged out, and got ready for my patient. A cold bottle of water on the end table for the client. A new client intake form for me. It was just a habit to have it with me. I never looked at the intake sheets anymore. I had all the questions memorized and I was good at remembering what we talked about.

When the elevator opened, I glanced at the clock on the wall. My patient was five minutes early. I took this as a good sign.

Since people tended to get turned around coming off the elevator, I went to the door.

This man, however, was walking right toward my office.

Maybe walking wasn't quite the right word. Sauntering was a more accurate word.

Tall and lean, he was handsome with a sexy five-o'clock shadow that many men would envy.

As he sauntered toward me, pulling off aviator sunglasses as he walked, he struck a feminine chord deep down in my reptilian brain. I recognized the way my heart rate sped up and butterflies took flight in my stomach.

He's a patient.

I tamped down those primitive feelings of attraction and gave him my most professional smile.

In the process of tamping down my attraction, I felt myself leaning toward the other end of the spectrum. Extremely professional.

"Come in," I said. "Have a seat."

Preview

Chapter 2

BENJAMIN Ashton

I valeted my rental car at my buddy Jonathan's office building and headed straight for the fifth floor.

I could have taken an Uber from the airport, but sometimes I just liked the challenge of navigating city traffic on a busy freeway.

Since I had been here when Jonathan moved into this office building, I was more than familiar with the layout.

The spacious lobby with tall ceilings and bright chandeliers would be intimidating to a lot of people, but Jonathan—Dr. Jonathan Baker—didn't worry about such things. He was going for the high-end clients and did so unabashedly. Ambition was his middle name and from what I could tell, he was doing quite well in that direction.

The building had tall imposing live green plants placed strategically around as well as oversized furniture where people could wait for their appointments or just sit and use the WIFI.

The building held all sorts of professional offices. It had a psychiatrist, a chiropractor, a whole floor for attorneys, and a floor for some kind of stock trading.

The rent in this place alone required a certain level of clients. Apparently Jonathan knew what he was doing. The last time I talked to him—about six months ago, maybe longer—he'd been talking about expanding his business. Hiring on some help.

Not a bad idea, but I recommended he put an attorney on retainer.

Not only did I come from a family of entrepreneurs located in Pittsburgh, but I worked for Noah Worthington of Skye Travels. Skye Travels was the premier private airline company in the country.

Noah had taken one small airplane and built a billion dollar company on his own. He was a legend in the field of aviation. New graduates lined up at his door to be interviewed. I was no exception.

I'd been lucky. He'd branched out to Pittsburgh, and was looking to hire a pilot for there.

Long story, but it was around that same time that I learned that Noah Worthington was actually my grandfather's brother.

So he was Uncle Noah. An odd turn of events that had turned out well. The two brothers had gotten reacquainted after having lost touch with each other for most of their adult lives.

It was hard to think of him as Uncle Noah. Instead, I mostly thought of him as the boss.

At any rate, I knew a little bit about starting and running a business.

The elevator that took me up to the fifth floor had that fresh clean scent that smelled like success.

I should have called him. He often worked late, doing paperwork, but it was possible he had a client at this late hour. It was okay. I didn't mind waiting.

I stepped off the elevator into a wide carpeted hallway and headed straight for his office. Realizing I still wore my sun glasses, I pulled them off and blinked as my eyes adjusted.

I nearly came to a stop and would have except that my feet had unstoppable momentum.

A young lady stood at Jonathan's door. Maybe he'd hired some help already.

"Come on in," she said. "Have a seat."

Not one to argue with a pretty girl, I did as she asked.

She was a petite thing, even in high heels, dressed in a professional skirt and blazer.

Professional down to the white collared shirt.

I followed her inside the office. I recognized the view and although the office had the same general arrangement, things looked different.

The couch was new. One of the chairs. White daisies on a vase on the desk. A candle throwing out a mixture of vanilla and cinnamon scent.

Definitely different from Jonathan's décor.

I decided to try out the couch.

She sat across from me, leaning forward, holding a clipboard on her lap.

"I'm pleased that you came in," she said.

"Me too."

"I'd like to start with some basic questions. Then we can see if we're a good match and set up a plan of treatment."

A good match, huh? That was one part I was feeling confident about. As far as a plan of treatment, that sounded a little out of my league.

I glanced over my shoulder.

"I was expecting Jonathan to be here."

"He and I work together," she said. He's just down the hall. Since he's booked ahead several weeks, I was hoping you would give me a chance to work with you."

I realized right then that I was at one of those crossroads that could be life-altering.

The sensation was a little like flying an airplane. I made decisions every day that I hoped led to the best outcome. I had learned to go with my instinct and not second-guess myself. It had served me well so far.

"Okay," I said, giving her a little smile.

"I should introduce myself. I'm Dr. Grace Miller."

I was headed down that slippery slope and although there was still time to jump off, I was intrigued enough to play along.

"Benjamin Ashton."

A brief flash of confusion flashed across her face, but was quickly gone. She didn't recognize my name.

"I don't know much about you," she said. "Your application answers didn't go much further than you being twenty-seven."

"I like my privacy," I said.

Since I was playing along, I decided to be as truthful as I could.

"I understand. So do I. I have just some basic questions to get out of the way. Questions that will help me get to know you better."

"Go ahead," I leaned back, getting comfortable, and stretched one arm out across the back of the couch.

I'd been on a lot of dates. Usually getting to know each other was a little more subtle. Maybe this was a better, more straightforward way to get acquainted.

"Let's start with your occupation."

"I'm a pilot," I said.

"I see. A commercial pilot?"

"I work for a private airline company based here in town."

"Skye Travels?" she asked.

"Is there any other?" I asked with a smile.

"Not that I'm aware of. Do you have any siblings?"

She hadn't so much as glanced at the clipboard in her lap.

"I have two older sisters, one older brother, and one younger brother."

"You have a really big family. What was that like for you? Growing up?"

"I had a good childhood. Our parents were strict, but fair."

"You were close to your siblings?"

"Mostly my younger brother, but we were all close."

"What about now?"

"Now?" I ran a hand along my chin. "Now they're all married."

"And you? Are you married?"

"I'm single."

She didn't even miss a beat. Talking to her reminded me in some ways of having a conversation with Jonathan. He was persistent also. Persistent and straightforward.

"What's it like being the only single person in your family?"

"They're all happy."

She leaned forward, looking into my eyes. Her eyes were a lovely shade of green. The color of a meadow seen from ten thousand feet in the bright sunshine of spring.

Her red bow shaped lips parted slightly, curved into a little smile that she seemed to be fighting a losing battle with. I could tell she was trying, rather unsuccessfully, not to smile.

"But what about you? What's it like for you?"

I shrugged.

"I now have two more sisters and two more brothers."

"You're close to your in-laws."

"We're all close. We all spend a lot of time together."

I opened my mouth to tell her that we all lived in the same house, but closed it. It wasn't something I told people quite simply because it was one of those things that was hard for people to understand.

It was hard for people to understand that our house was large enough to comfortably hold six families. Most people didn't even call it a house. They called it a manor—which it was.

I also didn't tell people that we had a cook, a gardener, and a housekeeper and all of them lived on the grounds.

Those were things I kept to myself.

"Tell me about your parents."

"They worked a lot, still do, but they always had time for us."

"They were supportive of your decision to become a pilot?"

I looked blankly at her a moment, then cleared my throat.

That was the other thing I didn't tell people. Not only did my uncle own the airline, but both of my brothers and both of my brothers-in-law were pilots.

"Yes," I said. "They are very supportive."

I was finding this conversation difficult. It was hard talking to her without telling her everything.

And even though there were things I didn't go around telling people, I wanted to tell her everything.

Preview

Chapter 3

GRACE

With the city ambiance that even drawn shades couldn't block out, I studied my new client.

I wanted to go back to my computer. I was decent at remembering names. I'd had it in my head that his name was Bradford... something. Not Benjamin. Maybe I'd read it wrong. But no. I distinctly remembered making a folder in the computer program with the name Bradford... something.

I'd straighten that out later. Couldn't very well jump up in the middle of a session to go to my computer because I was confused on his name.

So far I didn't see anything that would guide me toward a diagnosis. Jonathan would probably say he was enmeshed with his family, but I believed that to be a good thing. Families these days were too scattered and family support was one of those fundamental things that, in my experience, everyone needed.

When patients had family support, unless those families were completely dysfunctional, they typically fared much better than those who didn't have family support.

I had enough history from him for now. It was time to get some more pertinent information.

"Have you ever been hospitalized for mental health reasons?"

"No," he said.

"Have you ever had any kind of counseling?"

"No."

"You didn't indicate on your contact information anything that you might want to work on. Is there anything in particular that you'd like to talk about?"

He didn't answer right away. I gave him time to think. It was one of those thirty second pauses that seemed to last forever.

"It's just nice to have someone who listens."

If there was anything diagnosable about him, it was going to take some time to get him to talk about it. Private people were usually like that.

"It's hard for you to trust people," I said.

"I don't know if I'd go that far."

"But you don't have anyone you're comfortable talking to."

"I have a good friend. I talk to him."

"Yeah? When is the last time you spoke to him?"

"Christmas, I think. Maybe New Year's."

"So it's been about six months?"

"I guess so."

I wasn't concerned with that. It was typical guy behavior. Guys could go years without talking and still consider themselves good friends. When they picked up the phone, they just picked up the conversation like they had spoken last week.

It wasn't usually like that for women. I didn't like to generalize, but I saw it all the time. In order for girlfriends to remain girlfriends, they had to keep up with each other on a regular basis. Weekly. Sometimes even daily.

I had one friend, but he was a guy—also a graduate student.

Graduate school, then working didn't allow a lot of time for hanging out with friends.

The only people I'd gone out with socially during graduate school was fellow graduate students and all we talked about was psychology.

So I was in no place to judge Benjamin for going six months without talking to his best friend.

"What kinds of things do you do for fun?"

"I fly airplanes."

He said it without hesitation.

"I mean outside of your job."

"Occasional family time. A movie here and there. Grilling outside on family days."

"So no hobbies?"

"Flying is my hobby and my career."

"It's who you are."

"Yes." He sounded surprised that I understood that.

I knew what it was like to eat, sleep, and breathe one's career. It was what it took.

Having a career like psychology or aviation took complete focus.

My watch vibrated, telling me that we only had ten minutes left in the session.

"We only have about ten minutes left," I said. "So I'd like to go over what we talked about."

"Okay. Sure." He leaned forward and looked into my eyes. His eyes were a lovely deep cerulean blue that a girl could fall into.

How was it that a guy like this was still single?

Maybe that was something he wanted to work on.

"You're a pilot for Skye Travels. Flying is your passion. The one thing that's a constant in your life.

"You're close to your family. Two brothers, one older, one younger, and two older sisters. They're all married and you like their spouses. Am I right so far?"

"Impressively so."

"You have good family support and a good friend that you can talk to about just about anything. You're here because you just want someone to talk to."

"Yes," he said.

"Does this time and day work for you?"

He looked away for a moment. Gave me another one of those thirty second forever silences.

"I have an erratic schedule. I never know where I'll be."

"I can see where having someone to talk to could be a problem. Why don't you use the scheduling feature on the website to schedule your next session yourself. I'll recognize your name and I'll know you aren't a new client. Does that sound good to you?"

"It sounds okay to me," he said.

"So. Our time is up for now. Is there anything you'd like to add before you go?"

Clients invariably saved their true reason for coming to therapy for the last five minutes of the session. I always braced myself when I asked that question. I knew of psychologists had stopped asking for that very reason.

"Nothing to add," he said. "I enjoyed talking to you."

"Likewise."

He stood up from the couch and I stood up with him, holding my clipboard with both hands at my waist.

"Until next week then," he said.

"Next week. Whenever works for you."

"I'll let you know when I'm back in town."

"Take care, Benjamin," I said, walked to the door, and opened it.

"Good night," he said.

After stepping out into the hallway, I went back to my computer. I wanted to double-check his name. It wasn't like me to get the name of a new client wrong.

I went straight to the computer and logged in.

Ah ha. I had been right.

My client's name was Bradford.

And Bradford had sent an email asking to reschedule.

Preview

Chapter 4

BENJAMIN

I checked my watch as I stepped out of Dr. Miller's office.

I'd been in her office for fifty minutes, but it didn't seem like it. It seemed like I'd been there for about fifteen minutes. Time had flown by.

I stood in the hallway and considered. Jonathan had obviously moved his office. And he had obviously added someone into his fold. Just as he had said he would.

The problem at the moment was that I didn't know where to find Jonathan.

I walked to the end of the hall, checking names on doors as I went.

And there at the end of the hallway, I found his name on the door.

Dr. Jonathan Baker.

Since his door was closed, I sent him a text.

> Hey. I'm outside your new office.

He wouldn't answer if he was with a patient.

But he answered right back.

> JONATHAN
> I'm at the bar downstairs.

This day was just getting stranger and stranger.

> Do you want company?

> JONATHAN
> Sure. Come down.

Going back the way I came, I passed by Dr. Grace Miller's closed office. I was still a little dazed by that whole experience.

I had just gone through an entire counseling session.

I stopped, my hand almost to the elevator button.

Well hell.

I had just taken up an hour of her time that had been reserved for someone else.

That hardly seemed right.

I had to pay her for her time. For me the hour had been a casual interesting interlude, but for her, it had been work.

I never carried cash anymore, but I did keep one check on me for emergencies. I still, in this modern day and age, occasionally encountered someone who did not take credit cards, but oddly enough, would take a check.

Tugging the folded check out of my wallet, I wrote it out to her, leaving the amount blank, and signed it.

I wrote a note on the back.

I know I wasn't your scheduled client. Please fill in your rate for new clients.

I hesitated. I was running out of room, but I had so much I wanted to say. I boiled it down to the gist of it all.

Thank you for listening.

Feeling much better, I slid the check underneath her door and went straight to the elevator.

Maybe I'd have just one beer with Jonathan. It was early and I didn't have another flight until in the morning.

I needed to figure out just how much I was going to tell him about my hour with Dr. Miller.

Nothing. That's what I was going to tell him.

He'd probably tell me it was unethical pretending to be a client when I wasn't.

It wouldn't matter, or maybe it would make matters even worse, that I had enjoyed talking to Grace.

I got off the elevator, went outside, and walked across the street to the little bar where he and I had spent quite a few hours in our younger days. These days it wasn't like Jonathan to be here. He was typically home with his wife if he wasn't working.

But then again, as I had admitted to Grace, it had been six months since I had spoken to him. I had no way of knowing what was going on in his life right now.

He and I needed to do a better job of keeping up with each other.

I stepped into the upscale bar called simply *Equinox* and looked around for Jonathan.

The bar, a favorite hangout for the after work crowd was loud and the servers were hopping.

Jonathan, seeing me walk in, held up a hand and I spotted him across the room.

I slid into the booth across from him.

"What are you doing here?" I asked. "Why aren't you with Victoria?"

"Victoria left me."

Keep Reading Accidentally Forever...

Kathryn Kaleigh writes sweet contemporary romance, time travel romance, and historical romance.

kathrynkaleigh.com